Soul mate—or catastrophe?

The chaos of crunching metal, screeching brakes, plus the aroma of burning rubber is majorly distinct. It's like that chalk-shrieking-on-the-blackboard thing—only with cars. If you're hearing it without headphones? It means the front end of someone else's car has smashed into the back end of yours.

A split second after the moment of impact, I checked my vitals. The seat belt was in place, the air bags were deploy-challenged. Verdict: I wasn't hit hard. I took a deep breath and checked the rearview mirror. My makeup was stellar.

And then, in a tiny corner of the rearview, I saw him. The driver of the car that hit me. He sat there, stunned, gripping the steering wheel of an Acura SLX—only the sport utility vehicle of my dreams.

He was by far the cutest boy I had ever seen in real life. A studmuffin supreme.

Clueless® Books

CLUELESS™ • A novel by H. B. Gilmour
  Based on the film written and directed by Amy Heckerling
CHER'S GUIDE TO . . . WHATEVER • H. B. Gilmour
CHER NEGOTIATES NEW YORK • Jennifer Baker
AN AMERICAN BETTY IN PARIS • Randi Reisfeld
ACHIEVING PERSONAL PERFECTION • H. B. Gilmour
CHER'S FURIOUSLY FIT WORKOUT • Randi Reisfeld
FRIEND OR FAUX • H. B. Gilmour
CHER GOES ENVIRO-MENTAL • Randi Reisfeld
BALDWIN FROM ANOTHER PLANET • H. B. Gilmour
TOO HOTTIE TO HANDLE • Randi Reisfeld
CHER AND CHER ALIKE • H. B. Gilmour
TRUE BLUE HAWAII • Randi Reisfeld
ROMANTICALLY CORRECT • H. B. Gilmour
A TOTALLY CHER AFFAIR • H. B. Gilmour
CHRONICALLY CRUSHED • Randi Reisfeld
BABES IN BOYLAND • H. B. Gilmour
DUDE WITH A 'TUDE • Randi Reisfeld

Available from ARCHWAY Paperbacks

Dude with a 'Tude

Randi Reisfeld

AN ARCHWAY PAPERBACK
Published by POCKET BOOKS
New York London Toronto Sydney Tokyo Singapore

This book is a work of fiction. Names, characters, places and
incidents are products of the author's imagination or are used
fictitiously. Any resemblance to actual events or locales or persons,
living or dead, is entirely coincidental.

AN ARCHWAY PAPERBACK *Original*

 An Archway Paperback published by
POCKET BOOKS, a division of Simon & Schuster Inc.
1230 Avenue of the Americas, New York, NY 10020

® and Copyright © 1998 by Paramount Pictures

ISBN: 0-671-02090-0

First Archway Paperback printing August 1998

10 9 8 7 6 5 4 3

AN ARCHWAY PAPERBACK and colophon are
registered trademarks of Simon & Schuster Inc.

Printed in the U.S.A.

IL: 7+

Thanks to all the dudes and dudettes whose totally positive 'tudes went into making this book happen—specifically . . .

. . . Anne Greenberg at Pocket Books, who always has a "leg" up on everything cutting edge.

. . . flebowitz and Jason at Writers House, for hammering out the hard stuff and always E-ing there.

. . . Richard Alpern, Esq., and Irene Mecky, Esq. For being such the legal eagles.

. . . Scott Berchman, whose choice of dates is always inspirational.

. . . Always with love, gratitude, and pretzels, MR, SR, SR, and the Bo.

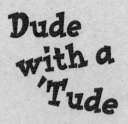

Dude with a 'Tude

Chapter 1

Mmm, another tasty idea, Cher!" My best friend, De, closed her eyes dreamily as she delicately bit into a super-size Mrs. Fields chocolate chunk cookie.

"Props accepted," I replied, washing my Cinnabon down with a double-decaf, low-fat, light-froth latte.

De and I were in the food court of the Beverly Center, a designer-enhanced mall that blends cutting-edge fashion with mass appeal. It's a place where Betsey Johnson coexists with Banana Republic, where Bauer (Eddie) meets Bisou (Bisou), and Joan & David nestle next to Timberland and Lady Foot Locker. It's the realization of that whole "I have a dream" thing that our parents marched for in the '60s. Or something.

And bonus, there's a M.A.C. boutique: makeup for the mind, body, and soul.

Our timing was titanic. We'd just taken the dreaded

PSAT test, which is brand name for the Preliminary Scholastic Aptitude Test. As high school juniors all over America know, they're frantically crucial. They allegedly pinpoint how you'll score on the SAT test, which fully foretells which college you'll get into, which determines the high-paying career you'll have, who you'll network with, where you'll shop, who you'll marry, what your children's names will be, where you'll live, and, hello, what car you'll drive.

In other words, your whole life fully depends on the PSATs.

A mere twenty-four hours ago, we'd been such the stress puppies. But now every last multiple choice had been number-two penciled in, and we were celebrating with a post-traumatic stress reduction shopping spree.

Because I'm the designated idea driver of our crowd, I'd come up with this megawatt lightbulb. Directly after the five-hour test—which began at the heinously early hour of 8 A.M.—we'd do a mall troll and accentuate with pit stops at selected junk-food nooks.

Then we'd signed up to attend a seminar of rampant relatability: The Love-O-Scope Solution: Your True Soul Mate. It was being given by world-famous astrologer Madame Tiara. We'd even bought tickets in advance to have our personal charts done. I'd cyber-submitted all pertinent information efficiently by uploading De's, mine, and Amber's personal Web sites onto Madame Tiara's very own loveplanets@horoscope.net site. Our Web sites tell everything about us, including physical description, birth dates, likes, and dislikes.

Serendipitously, the seminar was being held right

here, behind the for-ticket-holders-only velvet ropes in the food court. We'd positioned ourselves to score front-row seats, right next to the poster advertising Madame Tiara's in-person appearance.

Now, as the hustle and bustle of our excellently clad peer group buzzed around us and our filled-to-capacity designer shopping bags snuggled at our feet, our comfort level was stratospheric.

Except, of course, for the drag-down factor. Tragically, we always include Amber Marins in our plans, even though she's a fashion victim for the millennium and official third wheel. Whatever. Not even her tart-tongued sourness or her inane outfit—like who, besides Amber, would mix Power Ranger pink miniskirt with lizard skin cowboy boots?—could mar our post-test celebration.

"I can't believe how much better I feel," De sighed as she licked her finger and dipped it into those last few cookie crumbs on her napkin.

"And soon you won't believe how much chunkier you'll feel," Amber reminded her. "Just one cookie . . . so many sit-ups."

De glared at her. "Speaking of sit-ups, the reason you're sitting next to us would be . . . ?"

Amber, who'd eschewed the sweets-fest, ignored De's pointed diss. She needled, "Excuse me, like the PSATs are even remotely stressworthy? Dionne, sometimes I cannot believe the duh level of your priorities. Stress is when the waiter splashes the dressing *on* the salad, instead of on the side. Stress is when you have to squeeze the hairdresser, manicurist, personal trainer, masseuse, and tennis pro into one day and the chauffeur is delayed. And segue, even if we weren't bred to ace these pathetic standardized tests, options abound. Excuse me, who among us could not afford a major donation paving the way into the university of our choice?"

In tandem, De and I rolled our eyes. On the chutz-pah meter, Amber's reasoning never dipped below Herculean.

De challenged, "Of course, all that excess tutoring you had for the PSATs wouldn't have anything to do with your overconfidence overload?"

Amber had come to the test beyond prepared. Her parents had hired a plethora of private, top name, high-priced specialty tutors to eliminate any possibility of Princess choking when confronted with those tiny blank ovals.

Haughtily, Amber peered down her much-recon-structed nose at De. "As if I required help from the answer gremlins. Don't be naive. Sometimes in the game of life, one must appease the parental gods. I only agreed to the tutoring after careful negotiation with Daddy: a hundred bucks for every ten points over the median for our district."

She hit a button on her electronic organizer and smiled smugly. "Let's see. By this time next week when we get our scores back, I should be at least seven hundred dollars richer. Or in practical terms, two more of *these* babies"—Amber waved a catalog in our faces: the Manolo Blahnik of the Month Club—"will be joining the shoe and boot wing of my closet."

I sighed. What saved Amber from absolute delusion was this: she wasn't necessarily wrong. Past experience in the land of standardized tests *did* indicate our probable scores. No doubt I'll end up in the rampantly respectable ninety-ninth percentile, but Amber and De have a lock on top honors in our school. It's been that way on every national test, since like, preschool. Amber *should* rule the verbal portion of the PSATs, which measured vocabulary and reading comprehension. It was the one area where her barbed tongue actually served her well. And De will fully smash the myth that girls don't have the math gene. She'll rock.

Whatever. The point of *this* afternoon was not to rehash, but to let go. "Time to switch topics, girlfriends," I reminded them. "The PSATs are as over as CBS's attempt to steal the TGIF audience."

Just then another topic arrived to fill the void. A chicken-necked, beak-nosed, crone-esque woman— and I mean that in a wholly appropriate way—fully draped from head to ankles in layers of scarves and kerchiefs sailed past our table. I recognized her as the unairbrushed version of the woman on the poster: Madame Tiara was in the food court.

Attended by a pair of similarly clad assistants, the "As Seen on TV" astrologer ignored the waves of murmurs and pointing. She began setting up for her Love-O-Scope seminar. Efficiently, she instructed her assistants to prop up her visuals: a bunch of charts next to a colorful display of her books and inspirational tapes. All were for sale at the end of the session. I scanned the titles. *Madame Tiara's Soul Mate Search for Dummies, Madame Tiara's Rules,* and the hot-off-the-presses *Chicken Soup for Madame Tiara's Soul.*

I glanced around. The food court, only randomly populated when we'd first arrived, was now SRO. It was majorly buzzing with excitement. Clustered around tables was a mix of our peer group: the true believers, such as me and De; the horoscopically needy; and the just curious. Ringed outside the roped-off food court was another group: the "we're too cool for this, so we came to make fun of it" contingent. Primo examples of the latter were leaning against the wall by the rest rooms: De's boyfriend, Murray, and his number one homie, Sean. They were both in their traditional threads—skate pants, Hilfiger shirts, and colorful hats.

I nudged De's elbow. "Psst, don't look now, but your main boo is here."

De was less than amused. All week Murray had been ribbing her about the "Horror-Scope" seminar. She shot him a sharp "leave now" flash of her hazel orbs.

"Chill, De," I counseled. "Maybe Murray's really buggin'—he could be concerned about the possibility of astro-incompatibility between you two."

"If he was that concerned, Cher, he could have bought a ticket like the rest of us instead of heckling from the sidelines."

"That's severe, De. You know boys are viciously incommunicado when the topic is love. Murray's being here is just his way of saying he's searching, too. He shares your concerns."

Amber snorted. "Murray's here because he's afraid

De might suddenly realize what an insecure infant he is and decide to look elsewhere."

Again, Ambu-larva wasn't totally wrong. Murray's possessiveness was well documented. So was De's struggle to get him to loosen up. My opinion? Ambivalence prevails. A part of her rampantly revels in his pedestal-like worship; another part feels stifled.

All at once a hush fell over the food court. Madame Tiara cleared her throat and began her speech. "Welcome, seekers! Welcome!" She fully glowed, basking in the warmth of our sincere applause. Her wrinkled eyes danced as she encompassed everyone in her greeting. "I'm delighted to be here. For today we address a universal concern: love. Love is our deepest need. We all reach desperately for love, love with that one right person. For what is success, if we don't have the one right person to share it with? In astrology we call that person the twin soul—or soul mate. The enhancement of a life shared with a soul mate is a value beyond measure. It is the secret of life itself. So what if you can buy everything in this mall—what does it mean without love?"

Amber, who'd been on her cellular phoning in her catalogue orders, raised her hand.

Quickly, I pulled it down. "Rhetorical question alert, Ambu-dunce."

Murray and Sean found Madame's prologue stomach-grippingly hootworthy. De silenced them midhoot with another sharp glance.

Madame Tiara explained that her seminar would tackle the four most frequently asked questions: What is a soul mate? Does everyone have a soul mate? Is there only one soul mate for each of us? What is the Love-O-Scope way to find yours?

Naturally, Madame Tiara had the answers to all the above, but for a complete guide to the last one, we'd have to buy one of her books or tapes.

Over the next half hour, De and I gave her our undivided. Amber chose to resume multitasking instead. After a while, Murray and Sean bagged it. I guess boredom outweighed any insecurity Murray secretly harbored.

I was frantically unbored. Just the opposite—I found the seminar way inspirational. And furiously relatable. Not that my life has been hottie devoid. There have been a plethora of potentials. Like Aldo, the Italian exchange student; Bobby, the personal trainer; Matt, the photographer; Riccardo, the pool boy; Sonny, the age-inappropriate collegiate; Tony Trilling, the tennis pro—to alphabetically name a few.

But I had yet to find *the one*. Like where was the Tom to my Nicole? The John-John to my Carolyn? Even the Gavin to my Gwen—not that I'd ever consider putting that heinous dot on my face.

Finally, the public part of the seminar ended. It was time for those who'd paid in advance to learn their personal Love-O-Scope truths.

"Dionne Davenport," Madame Tiara sang out, "you're up first."

De rose and walked toward the astro-expert. Though De's confident strut is way famous at school, only a lifelong t.b. like me would sense her apprehension.

Like what if De found out she and Murray were astrologically doomed? Impulsively, I jumped up to follow her in case she needed support. Amber, mortified at being left out of anything, vaulted up, too.

De settled herself in a seat opposite the sun sign queen. Wasting no time, Madame Tiara smiled broadly and began reading from the chart she'd prepared based on the information from De's Web site. First, she detailed De's astro-profile. While I didn't understand all of it, on the upside De seemed to be "a bird with brilliant feathers, vivacious, clever, graceful, with disarming warmth and such a beautiful smile." My main was "a sunflower, not a wallflower, ridiculously popular, the social leader of her group. To your friends, you are fiercely loyal, kind, and generous. But your enemies should beware: your claws are sharp."

De was massively kvelling in her horoscope-of-perfection score.

But I was impatient. I already knew this stuff about De. At the risk of borderline rude, I interrupted, "What about De's soul mate? Who's right for her?"

Amber snorted. "Yeah, cut to the chase so she'll buy a clue and cut pathetic Murray loose."

De, faux annoyed, was just as anxious for her Love-O-Scope results.

Madame Tiara resumed studying the chart and then suddenly looked up. "Ah, your chart reveals a fiercely independent streak. You are not a docile little maid who hangs on your mate's every word. Your soul mate is masculine, strong, and secure. He knows you are a gem. He knows he's lucky to have you. He knows he must bring you gifts. You are a luxury item, not bargain basement."

Bottom line? De's true soul mate might seem meek on the outside, but he's totally tough on the inside. Like chenille. Or Murray.

"I'm next," Amber announced, tapping her Gucci timepiece impatiently. "My schedule is *muy* congested, and I've already spent more than the allotted time here."

Madame Tiara looked up, amused. "Amber Marins, I presume?"

Amber tossed her head back. "Presumption correct."

"How did you know?" I wondered.

Madame Tiara nodded gravely. "Ah, hers is a chart one remembers. Hers is a chart such as, in all my years as an astrologist, I have never come across. The rudeness, the impropriety, the superior attitude—who else could it be?"

Amber settled herself in the seat De had just vacated and prepared to be ego-stroked. Okay, so to anyone else, Madame Tiara's pronouncements would have been an ego-trashing, but to Amber's selective ears, it was way symphonic.

The astrologist intoned, "You, Amber Marins, due to a rare cusp-confluence of sun and moon ascendant, and fixed quadriplicity can often be"—it seemed difficult for her to continue, yet she did—"domineering, controlling, self-absorbed, and manipulating."

Amber glowed.

"Your life purpose is to creatively express the Self. You need to be appreciated for your uniqueness, freed from routine, given special attention. You are theatrical, grandstanding, intense, suspicious, vengeful, extreme."

Revelation: Amber's extreme fashion non-sense isn't even her fault. She's ruled by the zodiac gods.

Tentatively, I ventured, "So, who would Amber's soul mate be?"

De quipped, "Hello, who on this planet could put up with her—for life? Make that—for a life sentence."

Madame Tiara blanched. "The soul mate for Amber is docile, thrives on taking orders, has little self-esteem, and is easily manipulated."

Amber looked mildly suspicious. "What about his financial stats? C'mon, granny, I need deep pockets."

Madame Tiara went on. "Your soul mate, who appreciates your intense perceptions, sees you as deeply fascinating, agrees with all your choices, bows at the altar of your uniqueness."

Okay, so I saw it. Amber's true soul mate was . . . herself.

Finally it was my turn. Madame Tiara fished my chart out of the pile. "Cher Horowitz. It was a pleasure to do your chart, especially after hers." She nodded at Amber's swiftly disappearing back.

"You, Cher, are bold, daring, and passionate. You want to change the world. You're fair, gracious, beauty loving, kind, sensitive, analytical, a good negotiator. You are able to lead on behalf of good causes. Your life purpose is to fairly and gracefully reconcile opposites. You always see both sides of all issues—and you want to help."

I listened, fully astounded by the accuracy of Madame's depiction. I so am all those things—such the solution finder!

And then she unraveled one of my young life's most bodacious mysteries: the qualities my total soul mate would possess.

Later, as I drove along the palm-tree-lined boulevards of Beverly Hills, I mentally reviewed my main menu personality. Everything Madame Tiara had said rang majorly true, especially the description of my soul mate.

She'd said, "The soul mate for you, Cher, is your intellectual match. He possesses a sharp, intuitive mind. He appreciates you for your intelligence, your creativity, your generous spirit. He's romantic, a dreamer perhaps. He appreciates culture, he reads poetry. He can sometimes be sad and wistful. He shares your idealism, your passion about making the world a better place.

"Yet," she'd continued, "he will also be a homebody, a boy who will cook you a delicious meal, who will enjoy quiet nights by the fireplace."

When De heard that, she snorted. "Translation: he's cheap."

Not even. My true soul mate is intensely idealistic, profoundly passionate, deeply philosophical, rampantly romantic—such the highly evolved hottie. "It's not necessary," Madame Tiara had mentioned, "but if he's all those things, and born under the sign of Aries, he could be a keeper, Cher."

As I hung a louie into the majorly convoluted and construction-beleaguered intersection of San Vicente and Beverly Boulevard, my heart swelled with hope: the one soul mate for me is so out there.

I hadn't been given a physical description, but I'll know him when I see him. Could he not be a studmuffin supreme? He'll be stylish, but in an under-stated Istante way. His hair could be dark and wavy. Or blond and curly. His eyes would be piercing: the windows to his soul. When I see him, I'll see stars twinkling in the pink-tinged, smog-free skies. I'll so totally know when he's near. I'll hear music. Just like the song playing on the radio now, that Bryan Adams/Barbra Streisand duet, "I've Finally Found Someone." I'll hear . . .

CRASH!

Chapter 2

*O*ops. The chaos of crunching metal, screeching brakes, plus the aroma of burning rubber is majorly distinct. It's like that chalk-shrieking-on-the-blackboard thing—only with cars. It makes the hairs on the back of your neck bolt vertical. It creates full tummy turbulence, dread department. If you're hearing it without headphones? It means the front end of someone else's car has smashed into the back end of yours.

It isn't exactly the soundtrack I'd always imagined playing in the background the day I met my soul mate.

A split second after the moment of impact, I checked my vitals. The seat belt was in place, the air bags were deploy-challenged. Verdict: I wasn't hit hard. I took a deep breath and checked the rearview mirror. My makeup was stellar.

And then, in a tiny corner of the rearview, I saw him. The driver of the car that hit me. My hand flew to my mouth. He sat there, stunned, gripping the steering wheel of an Acura SLX—only the sport utility vehicle of my dreams.

He was by far the cutest boy I had ever seen in real life. A studmuffin supreme.

Instantly, I turned off the engine, flicked open my seat belt, de-Jeeped, and dashed toward him as quickly as my Joan & David strappy platforms could take me.

Inhaling deeply, he raked his fingers through his thick, black wavy hair and carefully emerged from his car. I took stock: he was tall, chiseled, buff—his Polo shirt was neatly tucked into Istante pants—and wedding ring devoid.

And like that famous poem about objects in the mirror being closer than they appear? Up close, he objectively appeared even cuter than in the mirror. If that was possible. He also appeared to be *majorly* buggin'. Salty little beads of sweat ringed his hairline.

He was shaken.

I was stirred.

"Are you okay?" I asked nervously, resisting the impulse to touch his hand.

He scoped me incredulously. Under eyelashes so long they should be illegal on boys, his eyes were the most intense shade of cobalt blue I had ever seen. He blinked. "Am *I* okay? I hit you! I should be asking you that question."

15

I checked myself up and down. "I seem to be intact," I replied coyly.

"Unfortunately, that can't be said of your car." He motioned to the mega-dent in the fender of my Jeep and took a step toward the spot where our cars remained connected. I inspected the damage. He was right, my car *had* borne the brunt of our metallic interface. His had but minor bruises.

"Look," he breathed nervously, running his slender fingers through his dark silky locks again, "I'm really sorry. This is all my fault."

"Not even," I replied forcefully. I flashed on that "sees both sides of all issues" trait of my astro-profile. "Potentially, it was mea culpa. I might have stopped brutally short, giving you no choice but to lip lock me . . . I mean that in a vehicular sense, of course."

The trace of a grin started to form on his macho mug, but he quickly stifled it. "That's awfully sweet of you, but I can't believe that's what happened. It was probably some delayed signal I didn't see. I was looking for a street sign . . ."

"Looking for a street sign?" I repeated, curious. "Where were you going?"

"Home. That is, I just moved to Beverly Hills and wasn't sure if San Vicente crossed with Sunset. Look, uh . . . Miss . . ."

Impulsively, I thrust out my hand to shake his. "Horowitz. Cher Horowitz. And you would be . . ."

"Jake Forrest." He took a deep breath and glanced around. We'd unintentionally created this, like, major traffic dustup. Our cars now blocked the right lane, so traffic had to divert around us and squish together into the left lane—which just happened to be a turn-only lane. It wasn't making our fellow motorists happy.

"So, Jake Forrest," I continued, determined not to be distracted by the rude gestures and blaring horns, "you're new in Beverly Hills?"

Jake glanced around, unsure of the appropriateness of like, exchanging pleasantries, when all around us car-commotion reigned. But when he peered deeply into my baby blues—like thank you, M.A.C. makeup gods—I had his undivided.

He coughed self-consciously and tried to avert eye contact. It was such the defense mechanism so I wouldn't realize he was attracted to me. "I actually just moved from San Diego a week ago. I transferred to, uh, UCLA."

UCLA stands for University of California at Los Angeles. It's a way righteous, academically select, geographically desirable institution of higher learning that straddles the border of Beverly Hills and West-wood. It's also, like our next-door college. Translation: Jake is age- *and* zip-code appropriate.

"Which dorm are you in?" I prompted, fishing for the full 411.

"I'm not in a dorm. My mom and I moved into—"

Just then the thunderous blare of a car horn brutally interrupted our conversation.

"Move it," bellowed a distressed driver as he shot out from behind Jake's car. "Pull over to the side!"

His companion taunted, "Call the traffic cops! Whatsa matter, blondie, you cell phone deficient or something?"

"As if!" I responded, insulted at that last suggestion. All around us, cars continued to honk. Like did they even know how distracting that was? How could I begin to get Jake's digits, how could I suggest we get together again amidst all that noise?

Just then another car came swerving out of the intersection and pulled up next to us. I recognized the heinous hues of a squad car. Out popped a member of the Beverly Hills police force. Tragically, it was a familiar one.

The chipmunk-cheeked Officer Krupke and I have crossed paths before. Usually, it's the fault of those totally random four-way stop signs all along Beverly and Rodeo Drives. He doesn't share my view of them as merely suggestions.

But my relationship with this paunch-prone career cop extends beyond my sporadic pause-deficiency. My daddy, Mel Horowitz, is a totally prominent Beverly Hills attorney who's been profiled in *People* magazine. Officer Krupke sometimes lends his expertise on Daddy's cases. He's such the detail-drone that Daddy dubs him "Special K: my ace in the hole." Addendum: They're also friends.

"Cher!" He shot me a concerned look. "Are you okay? What happened?"

Jake and I verbally tripped all over each other assigning self-blame. Officer Krupke's bushy eyebrows shot up. He looked stunned. I knew exactly what he was thinking: like hadn't Daddy taught me better than to accept fault when someone else was clearly in the wrong?

"I guess we should exchange . . ." Jake, fidgeting for his wallet, started.

"Digits," I responded, fishing in my Tignanello snakeskin slingback for paper to write down my phone numbers—cellular and home.

Officer Krupke folded his arms across his chest, amused. "Cher? I think what this young man means is that you need to exchange insurance information. You had an accident—you need to report it. That's the way it works here in the real world."

I waved him away. "Hello? I *know* that, Officer K. We were getting to that. But there's no serious rush. No one was hurt. And the damage to my car is furiously fixable."

Officer Krupke shot me a stern look. "Insurance information, both of you, *now*. And, Cher, go turn the motor on, make sure your car is drivable."

The long arm of the law had spoken. Or something. I sighed and walked back to my car. When the ignition kicked in, I drove forward a few feet. The car seemed roadworthy, and the insurance info was where it belonged, in the glove compartment.

When I reemerged, Jake seemed discombobulated. Apparently, the license, registration, and insurance card he'd handed the officer weren't like, currently kosher or something. He flipped through the cards in his wallet, mumbling, "I'm in the process of switching addresses and—"

Officer Krupke looked dubious. But before he could say something *NYPD Blue*-ish, I interjected, "Look, Officer K, this young man only just moved here. Like his papers could even *be* in full working order already? Not even. I'll take responsibility for dealing with this later."

Flushed with relief, Jake smiled. My knees went fully weak. I had to grip the side of my car to keep from falling over, for the dimples he displayed were as deep as, well, the dent in my back fender. And maybe it wasn't the right time, but his eyes sparkled. "Listen, Cher," he said, "I'll pay . . . that is, my insurance company will pay for any damage. You shouldn't have to assume responsibility for this. I will."

Jake was being amazingly sweet. I had to get Officer Krupke off his case.

"Look, Officer. This motor mishap is on the no-fault line. And once Jake gets his paperwork together, we'll file with the insurance company. Don't wig—we'll do our civic duty."

Jake bit the corner of his lip and peered at the sidewalk. "I really appreciate you being so understanding about this. I'll call you, Cher, okay? And we'll straighten this out. I promise."

What I wanted to say was, "Call me the minute you get home!" I wanted to shout, "I can't wait to hear from you again!" But what I said as I slipped back into my car was, "I know you will."

The last words I heard before I drove away were Officer Krupke's. "This is contrary to procedure. I don't like this, Cher. And your father isn't going to, either."

He was right.

My daddy, Mel Horowitz, doesn't usually do sulky. He gets paid big bucks to pummel his opponents in court, but at home he's putty. Silly sometimes, indulgent, cheerful, and way understanding, especially when it comes to me.

We have a special bond. It's been just the two of us since Mom died, during Madonna's ill-conceived disco period. Daddy and I totally rely on each other. He supports my spending habits, and I keep Casa Horowitz humming along smoothly. I schedule his charity balls, chiropractor appointments, and compulsory visits with aging relatives. But I'm more than the diva of the domicile. I'm chronically competent in the workplace as well. While I have no interest in following in Daddy's lawyerly footsteps, still, I am his top choice as junior assistant on some of his research-intense cases. I'm majorly adept at circling, highlighting, and underlining stuff.

All of which Daddy takes into account whenever I max out the credit cards or break curfew. It was the kind, understanding, indulgent Daddy I expected to encounter as I reported on today's majorly minor fender-bender.

So how could I even guess that by the time I got home, Daddy had a front row seat at Club Grumpy?

For the Daddy I spied as I bounced into his wood-paneled study was hunched over his desk, fully absorbed in a messy mound of paperwork. I leaned over and planted a kiss on his forehead. "Bad posture alert, Daddy," I reminded him gently. "Use the lumbar support pillow that's attached to your chair—your back will thank you in the morning."

Instead of favoring me with his usual adoring smile, Daddy shot me a brief, "Uh-huh." He ignored my posture recommendation.

I pushed some papers aside and hopped up on a corner of his desk. "Hey, Daddy, guess what happened today?"

His brow furrowed. He sighed and mumbled, "I'm not really in a guessing mood, Cher." His eyes never strayed from his desk, except to reposition the papers I'd disturbed.

Clue: It's possible he may not react with his usual understanding to the car-bumping incident. Yet I had to confess. I chose a circuitous route. "Okay, so I'll tell you. I think I aced the PSATs."

Daddy nodded. "Uh-huh."

"And then I got my astrological chart done."

Daddy didn't look up, just dittoed, "Uh-huh."

I calculated. Would that be his reaction no matter what I said? I could live with "uh-huh." In fact, "uh-huh" might be a good thing—if he stayed with it. I took a deep breath and delivered the fender-bender bulletin.

Tragically, grievously, heinously, he didn't stay with the "uh-huh" theme.

Instead, Daddy's head jerked up. His eyes filled with

22

fear. "You had a car accident? Are you all right? Should we call Dr. Limpkin?"

I tilted my head and went reassuring. "Tscha, Daddy, I'm fine. It was such the stroke of good planning that my car is industrial strength. It absorbed the brunt of the damage."

But instead of the total relief Daddy should have exhibited, his expression betrayed suspicion. It wasn't good when he bolted up and marched out of his study. By the time I caught up with him, Daddy had flung open the front door and was in the driveway, circling my car.

Suddenly, Daddy had on his courtroom voice. "Tell me what happened, Cher. The evidence suggests someone ran into you."

I didn't want him to get a bad impression of Jake. So I blamed the circumstances.

"It was majorly chaotic. Between the road construction, disappearing lanes, and those heinously orange cones—like, segue, who chooses those colors?—it was like that crash-test-dummy obstacle course. I was fully focused, but I might have braked brutally. The car behind me didn't have enough room to stop. Before he hit me, that is."

Daddy didn't buy it. Shaking his forefinger at me, he played the assumption card—assumptions based on living with me for the past seventeen years. "You were daydreaming, weren't you, Cher. Young lady, if you can't pay attention when you're driving, you don't deserve a license!"

"I wasn't daydreaming," I protested. "I was thinking about . . . the future."

Daddy glared at me. "When you're behind the wheel of a car, you think about the present—and the traffic, the signals, the construction if necessary, and yes, you watch where those orange cones are placed! Period."

Punctuation aside, that wasn't the end of Daddy's run-on rant. "Where were you coming from anyway? And please, *please* don't say the mall."

I didn't say anything.

Daddy had ramped onto the postal parkway, and he was way above the speed limit. He did that thing where he starts marching in one direction, then brutally flips around and marches the other way. His head shakes from side to side. "The mall again! You live there! For heaven's sake, Cher, the car could be on auto pilot and find its way home. So don't give me any excuses about some confusing intersection."

Those tiny little veins on the side of Daddy's forehead bulged. I felt a swatch of guilt about causing him so much stress. I tried to think of a way to soothe his temper, but things only got worse as Daddy probed further. Especially when I confessed that I hadn't gotten Jake's insurance 411. Yet.

"You didn't *what?*" Daddy's pitch matched a Celine Dion power screech.

Then he went all litigator and trashed my defense.

"You had a good feeling about him? And that's why you just let him drive off? How could you do that?

What exactly is to stop him from disappearing and never contacting you?"

I shuddered. But not for the reason Daddy thought I did.

"Cher, I'm disappointed in you. You handled this situation poorly."

Daddy wasn't calmed when I offered that Officer Krupke was on the scene. In fact, that's when he went atomic. "A police officer was on the scene—a friend of the family—and you didn't let him protect you? What's wrong with you?"

Heinously? Like if it was even possible? Things spiraled out of control after that. Daddy totally went off on me about spending too much money, daydreaming, and not taking responsibility for my actions. He implied that I might have to use my allowance to pay for the damages on the car. He was convinced Jake would bail.

I decided to let the defense rest. When Daddy gets like this, it's better to stay silent and simply mime facial remorse.

During a pause in his blame-o-rama, I bolted upstairs to my room. At the sixth step, it hit me: Daddy's overreacting to my minor motor infraction is unusual but not an isolated incident. He's been a regular at Club Crabby lately. I didn't know why.

But maybe it's his study—he's been spending a bodacious amount of time there. I made a mental note to call a feng shui master to rearrange his office. Knocking out some walls, adding a window for eastern exposure could go a long way toward soothing Daddy's frayed edges. His back *and* his daughter would benefit.

But as I flung myself down on my queen-size bed and reached for my phone, the call I made wasn't to the feng shui institute on Wilshire. Like, priorities! An hour ago I'd bumped into my potential soul mate—I had to call De.

She picked up on one ring, and I burbled with excitement. "You will never guess what just happened to me on the way home, girlfriend!"

De ventured, "You passed the Anna Sui boutique on Little Santa Monica and found the suede strappy platforms to go with the satin sheath dress."

"Better."

"You found a bag, too?"

"De! I'm totally serious here."

"Hello, Cher, so am I."

"Dionne, brace yourself. I think I met my soul mate!"

De gasped. I could practically see her eyes widen in surprise. "On the way home from the Love-O-Scope seminar? That is beyond fated, Cher."

"I know—I can barely believe it myself."

"Describe!" De commanded.

I didn't leave any parts out. Only when I'd finished, the edge was off De's excitement. My true blue withheld full enthusiasm. She even contradicted my postscript about how Jake and I had "met cute."

Instead, she snorted, "Only *you* could call a car accident 'cute,' Cher."

I refused to be excitement-derailed. "Random accident? Or cosmic collision? Dionne Davenport—*you* make the call."

She sighed. "Maybe I will, Cher. In time. But let's review what we know so far. You met this dude five seconds ago. The sum total of your experience with him is A) he slammed into your car and, B) drove away without following the law-abiding course of giving you his insurance information. And the survey says: you'll excuse me if I can't wrap 'soul mate' around my brain just yet."

I was piqued. "Like, grrrrr! Your lecture is off base, girlfriend, and tardy. I already got that from Daddy. What about my instinct here? Jake will fully live up to his lawful obligations. And then the only thing he'll be guilty of stealing is my heart. And I'll fully comply with that. Just wait and see."

27

Chapter 3

After I hung up with De, I was seized by the overwhelming need for a bubble bath. I checked my Movado: 6:30 P.M. Two thoughts came to me. The first: It had been like over an hour and Jake hadn't called. I pushed that one into the background and acted on the second, a more favorable one. I had just enough time to order dinner from Wolfgang Puck's Café and luxuriate in my bath before it was delivered.

Still, I took the cellular *and* the cordless into the bathroom—just in case.

Tragically, Jake didn't call, but the incense and aromatherapy candles I lit did the trick. By the time I emerged, I was relaxed, calm, moisturized, and secure. De and Daddy were furiously wrong to be suspicious. I was rampantly right to be optimistic, to believe in fate.

Doesn't Daddy always advise, "Go with your gut"? Well, hello, my gut tells me Jake will prove fully upstanding—and more. Then my gut suddenly sent another message: ping, I'm starving!

As soon as the front door chimes rang announcing dinner delivered, I dashed downstairs. With Daddy's mood in mind, I'd ordered his favorite, the calorically overloaded chicken parmesan. It's too down-market to actually appear on the menu. But in deference to Daddy's status as the most respected attorney-to-the-stars in Beverly Hills, Wolf whips it up special for him. He even agrees to label the side dish "spaghetti" instead of pasta.

For myself, I ordered seared ahi tuna and lobster ravioli, a dish that might be borderline overexposed, but a classic nevertheless. As I prepared dinner—that is, pulled the recyclable lids off the microwavable containers—I thought about Daddy's overreaction to my traffic bad. I decided to make a strong motion that he reevaluate and do that sentence suspended thing.

But it was all motion denied.

Grievously, when I finally coaxed Daddy to the table, he remained profoundly prickly. Against every Zone rule, he began to furiously inhale his dinner. The comfort food fest had not comforted Daddy in the least.

All at once I had a revelation: maybe Daddy's season's pass to Club Crabby wasn't about me. Maybe it was rooted in something else. But what? There was one surefire way to find out. Guilt him into it.

"Daddy," I began. My voice oozed with concern. "I feel so *majorly responsible* for your angst. What can I do to relieve your pain?"

Daddy glanced at me, still irritated. He put his fork down. "Ask not, Cher, what you *can* do to relieve my pain—listen up as I now dictate what you *will* do."

I didn't show it, but inwardly? Total panic. Partial coopting of famous verse is way unlike Daddy. So is his use of the secretarial word "dictate." Wisely, I placed down my own fork and tilted my head remorsefully.

It had no impact as Daddy decreed, "For starters, Cher, the credit card hemorrhaging ends now. You will cease and desist all shopping until every last penny of the repairs on your Jeep are paid for. Tomorrow morning you will take responsibility and drive the car to the repair shop."

I solemnly nodded. "That is so done, Daddy."

Naturally, I assumed Daddy would be proud of me for not arguing with him. Assumption like, overruled. Daddy was all, "You think that's going to be easy? You think car repairs come cheap? You're about to get a long overdue lesson in the real world. Where money, contrary to your experience, does not sprout from palm trees."

Daddy's use of that Jurassic "money doesn't sprout from trees" expression only strengthened my belief that he was displacing. While accepting full punishment—like I knew Jake would come through, so it was a no-brainer to just say "done deal"—I insisted on gently probing further.

"Daddy, you are so justifiably wiggin' over my fender bender, but I can't release the feeling that this goes deeper. You haven't been your cheerful self in weeks. Are you going all midlife crisis-y? Because if you are, they're doing some amazing things with feng shui . . ."

Daddy scowled. "Midlife crisis? Ha! I wish it were that clichéd."

He does? Okay, *now* I was awash in terror. To someone in midlife, there's only one thing worse than midlife crisis. What if Daddy's really sick or something? What if I'm about to go all Little Orphan Annie? Would I have to curl my hair? And color it that heinous shade of red?

With the song "Tomorrow" playing in my head, I gulped. "Whatever it is, you can tell me. I'm old enough to hear it."

Suddenly, Daddy's face drained of all color. He heaved this major sigh and leaned back in his chair. "Has it been that obvious, Cher? I'm sorry."

"As obvious as Jenny McCarthy's roots. I know when something bad is majorly buggin' you out. Is it . . ." I sputtered, ". . . your heart?"

Daddy looked stunned. "Wha-a-t? You think I'm sick? Oh, Pumpkin, I'm sorry. I'm fine. I didn't mean to worry you." After the obligatory, "You don't need to be concerned," and "It's no big deal," Daddy finally shared. Partially, that is.

And I was right: it *wasn't* about me. Apparently, his whole grump demeanor was work related. Some heinous blast-from-the-past lawsuit had come back to haunt him.

My panic subsided. "Tscha, Daddy! If it's just some yucky old case dragging you down, I can help. I'm so here for you. Just show me the highlighters. Dump the papers on me. I'll circle dates, phone numbers, addresses, cell phone calls, even the ones from roaming areas . . ."

Daddy tried for a dental display but managed only weariness. "I know you're here for me, Cher, and I know you want to help but—"

Just then our front door chimes rang. I wondered if it was De, here in person to rag on me for believing in fate. Or Murray, sent by De to rag on me. Or maybe even Amber, her antennae up for something good that happened to me and not her.

But when Daddy returned from answering it, the person with him was so not one of my friends.

Clad in Dockers and an athletic gray Gap T-shirt, he peered at me from under a backward baseball cap. I wondered what he was delivering.

Daddy cleared his throat. "Cher, this is Adam Gardner."

Though I couldn't imagine why a new gardener would show up on a Friday night, I smiled encouragingly. "The lawn's in furious need of an overhaul, but you'll be able to see that better in the daylight."

Daddy and Adam did a tandem double-take. Then Daddy burst out laughing. "No, honey, he's not the *gardener,* that's his name—Adam Gardner."

Gamely, I tried to cover my gaffe. "I bet you get that all the time, people mixing up your last name with a service-intense profession."

Instead of politely agreeing, Adam eyeballed me. His hazel eyes flicked with amusement. "Not really. Not ever, in fact. This is a first."

Okay, *don't* let me off the hook. What*ever*. I shrugged. "My bad."

Daddy jumped in to explain. "Adam's a prelaw student at UCLA. I brought him in to assist with research on the Heller case."

I'd never heard of the Heller case. Unless it was . . .

My blank expression prompted Daddy to add, "That's the case I just started to tell you about. The one that's sent me to, as you would say, Club Grumpy."

I know Daddy meant that "as you would say" benignly, but with Adam here, it felt condescending. I started to feel icky all over, especially after Daddy invited Adam to join us. My icky feelings morphed to beyond nauseous when the brown-nose prelaw student totally ogled what was left of Daddy's dinner.

"Is that chicken parmesan?" he asked, feigning incredulous. "It looks great. Cher must be some cook."

"As if!" I fumed.

Daddy nearly choked on his spaghetti.

Like, how'd I suddenly get relegated to such the girly-girl isn't-she-a-great-cook position? What's *that* about? My eyes flaring, I informed him coolly, "Dinner is courtesy of Wolfgang Puck's Café, only the most cutting edge celebratorium east of Doheny Drive."

Adam, unimpressed, slid into the chair on Daddy's left. "Oh yeah, I've heard of that one. What do they charge—twelve dollars for a turkey sandwich or something? Too rich for my blood."

My own blood started to boil as Daddy like, not only agreed with this style-challenged interloper, but asked me to go to the kitchen and get a plate for Adam.

When I returned to the table—with a plate *and* a glass, thank you—Daddy and Adam were already discussing the Heller case. I listened for a sec, then interrupted. "You know, Daddy, I'm wholly available to help, too."

Daddy flipped around to me, his fork in midair. Again, it felt all condescending when he said, "I know that, sweetie, but this case is a bear. It's really complicated."

Adam's eyes were downcast. Fighting a smile, he pushed his portion of spaghetti around with his fork. I felt like pointing out that only children play with their food. To Daddy I responded, "Excellent. The more complicated, the better. I could start tonight, even."

Daddy patted my hand paternally. "That's not necessary. C'mon, Pumpkin, it's Friday night. I know you've got better things to do than hang around with your old man, going over some boring files from a decade ago. Where are your friends tonight, Cher?"

I was just about to jump up and shout, "Stop treating me like some insipid teenager! I'm just as capable of helping you as this . . . this . . . faux lawn-care person. This Adam. I can do this! I want to do this!"

But I didn't say any of that, because just then my cellular rang.

It was Jake.

I excused myself and ran to my room to take the call.

The last thing I heard before dashing up the stairs was Daddy telling Adam, "Thanks for coming out on a

Friday night. I normally wouldn't ask that of my interns. But this lawsuit just blindsided me. Never expected it."

At the sound of Jake's voice, my spirits soared. He had so *not* hit and run. How very vindicating.

Okay, so he didn't precisely have the whole insurance thing settled yet. But Jake had something better: the same feelings I did.

It was so cute the way he went all tentative. "I know I should have waited to call you. I know it's been only a few hours. But I held out as long as I could. Look, Cher, I hope you don't think this is out of line, considering the circumstances. But here's the thing . . ."

He took a deep breath and delivered. "I'd really like to see you again."

Under normal conditions, at this point in the conversation I'd go coy. It's a golden rule of teen dating: never let a boy see you pant. But with Jake? The Rules went out the bay window.

Softly, I admitted, "I'd like to see you again, too, Jake."

There was silence on his end, though I thought I heard a huge sigh of relief. Quickly I added, "Provided, of course, you, uh, well, the car accident thing really has my dad buggin'. So we *will* get that straightened out, right?"

"Of course!" Jake exclaimed. "Your dad isn't the only one who went haywire. You should have heard my mom. She chewed my head off!"

My heart swelled. Jake understood. He, too, was mired in parental postal.

"It so boggles the way parents go ballistic over the trivial," I said empathetically. "Like they don't trust us to deal with stuff."

Jake agreed wholeheartedly. Then he got back to the heart of the matter. "Um, about going out. I know this is short notice, and please don't be insulted, but would tomorrow be too soon?"

Too soon? Not even. Before I could answer, Jake offered, "I don't know Beverly Hills all that well, but I've heard about this awesome observatory—"

"Griffith Park," I interjected knowingly. It's a place immortalized in an archival movie for its romantic sweeping vistas. Jake probably read about it in some tourist guide. Not being a native he couldn't know that like, no one schleps up there anymore—except tourists.

"Griffith Park, that's it," he said brightly. "Would that be okay? Maybe we could have a picnic lunch or something?"

A picnic lunch? I bit my lip. I couldn't remember any boy ever even suggesting that. It sounded . . . quaint. Like something out of Grandma Ray's time. I wondered if Jake was some sort of retro freak. Taking my silence for negativity, he amended, "Sorry. You probably think that's a dorky idea. Forget it. We can do something else."

Major oops. I'd made Jake feel bad already. The poor guy probably thought he'd come up with some rampantly romantic plan, and I'd reacted with as much enthusiasm as audiences had for Janet Jackson's last album.

I rewound. "No, no—Griffith Park is a way righteous selection. But it's not in Beverly Hills. And since you're a newbie, why don't I show you around? Then we can go to Griffith Park if you want."

Jake didn't hesitate. "You sure? I mean, that would be great."

"Then it's settled. Why don't you come by . . ." I was about to suggest that right this minute would be not a minute too soon, when I remembered two things: I needed time to prepare for our first date, and, real world intrusion, I had to deal with my car. I explained about the Daddy-decreed repair shop thing and suggested Jake come by in the afternoon.

Jake went proactive. "I have a better idea, Cher. What if I follow you to the repair shop? You'll need a ride back, anyway. We can leave from there."

Chapter 4

Displaying an admirable sense of on-timeliness, Jake showed up at precisely eleven the next morning. His studmuffin looks were no figment of my frazzled fender-bender imagination. If anything, he was even hotter than he'd seemed yesterday. He'd done this total Tommy casual thing, all multihued primary colors. While De and I ordinarily frown on mono-designer statements, on Jake's rockin' bod it worked.

Especially with the accessory he was grasping: one perfectly petaled, bodaciously brilliant, butternut yellow sunflower.

I melted. "For me?"

He blushed and averted full eye contact. "I wasn't sure what to bring. A bouquet seemed so . . . unoriginal. But at the florist I saw this." He shrugged adorably. "It reminded me of you. I hope you don't think it's cheesy."

I reached out to take it from him. "Sunflowers are my favorites, Jake."

He lit up. "They are? All *right!*" He followed me into our marble-tiled, domed entryway.

"I'll put this in a vase and then I'll be ready."

As I disappeared into the kitchen, I could feel Jake's eyes following me. I wasn't surprised when he called out, "You look . . . wow. I mean hot, Cher."

I did, too. It had taken me like, all night to settle on *the* ensemble. I was viciously hampered without De. Deciding on style choices for important occasions is something we traditionally do together. But she'd begged off to spend the evening with Murray, celebrating a PSAT-stressless weekend together.

Even without her help, my eventual choice of a short-sleeved baby blue cashmere top and DKNY flat front pants was stellar. Best of all, it meshed conceptually with Jake's red, white, and Tommy blue. He was the classic Kodak to my Polaroid of perfection.

Only one tiny wrinkle marred the moment: Daddy was AWOL. I so wanted him to meet Jake to see that he wasn't some hit-and-run felon. But my workaholic parental unit had left early that morning to pick up Adam. They'd gone to some storage vault downtown to unearth some of Daddy's old case files.

I put the sunflower in a vase and planted it on the dining room table. Then Jake jumped in his Baltic blue Acura SLX and followed me to the Beverly Hills Body

Shop. At first I couldn't understand why Daddy would direct me to that famous fragrance emporium, but like, doy, this turned out to be a shop for my car's body.

When we got there, Jake gallantly explained to the repair dude—whose name, Hal, was stitched onto the pocket of his shirt—that he'd have the insurance quagmire straightened out early in the week.

Hal was like, what*ever*. He took copious notes on his clipboard pad as he circled my Jeep, expressionless. I couldn't understand why he was writing so much. Finally he said, "This'll run ya fifty-three hundred dollars, give or take a few hundred."

I was startled. "Five thousand . . . you mean, dollars? That could buy an entire Dolce & Gabbana ensemble, accessories included! How could it cost that much to undent this tiny little fender bruise?"

Hal shrugged. "Parts."

I took that to mean everything was a la carte. I was right.

Hal continued, "I gotta get parts. You gotta replace the fender. Nuts. Bolts. Plus labor, naturally."

Jake squeezed my shoulder reassuringly. I took a deep breath and regained my composure. "Well, um, okay. I mean . . . I guess, whatever. The insurance company will fully reimburse you."

Hal took the keys from me and started to walk away. "I don't care where the check comes from, girly, just so long as someone has it ready for me in three weeks, give or take. An' don't forget the deductible."

40

Hal was deducting something? Righteous.

As I hopped into the buttery soft gray leather bucket seat of Jake's car, I calculated, "Three weeks. That's like an eternity to be immotorized."

Jake sighed. "This is my fault, Cher. I'll make it up to you. I'll take you everywhere you need to go until you get your car back."

I totally tingled at his above and beyond gesture. "That's sweet, Jake, but furiously impractical. You need your car to go to classes. And, I guess, for your social life."

Okay, that tacked-on part *was* fishing. But, hello, Jake wanted to be caught. He turned away from me, a little embarrassed, and murmured, "I was sort of hoping *you* would be my social life, Cher."

I flashed a major grin.

He brightened. "So, tour guide—where to?"

I pointed. "Well, if you make a left at the next light, we could head toward Rodeo Drive. It's our most indigenous boulevard. Home to designer boutiques both classic and cutting edge."

Jake listened intently and kept his cobalt blue eyes on the road as he followed my directions. I sneaked a sidelong glance at him. His square jawline, noble nose, and furiously full lips suggested the cover of a J. Crew catalogue.

When he noticed my stare he blushed.

Embarrassment oops. Quickly, I tried to cover up. I grazed my hand over the intense leather seats. "Mmm, smooth," I ventured. "This car has serious next on my dream list. It's like the only sport ute that comes equipped with necessary accessories. Like a safari-size power moon roof. And a six-disk CD entertainment unit. And this . . ."

I lifted the humongo fold-down armrest that separated us and continued, ". . . a center console with a triple beverage holder. Enough space for lattes, cosmetics, and . . ."

I peeped inside, and, and, he*llo,* how weird was this? Stuffed in Jake's center console was a vintage issue of *People* magazine. But not just any issue. It had "sexiest man" George Clooney on the cover. And inside? This ragin' profile of Mel Horowitz, primo attorney to A-list stars. And, sidebar—like, literally—there was a picture of me with Daddy and some stuff about me, stylish daughter to the primo attorney to the stars. It mentioned my favorite designers and that I have my own Web site.

I shot Jake a quizzical. "Is there something you want to tell me?"

"Huh?" Jake seemed flummoxed. "About what?"

I flashed the magazine at him. "This. Why is this in your car?"

Jake shrugged. "Uh, because my mom sometimes leaves her junk in the car? Is there something wrong, Cher?"

"So, you never read this?"

"Probably not. I don't usually read generic celebrity magazines. That's Mom's thing. Me, I'm more of a *Sports Illustrated* and *Rolling Stone* kinda guy."

I mused, "So you don't know that this issue has an article about Daddy? And . . . me?"

Jake swerved into the parking lane and hit the brakes abruptly. He seemed stunned. "It does? Are you someone famous?"

I went coy and opened to the article. "In certain circles . . ."

The palm of Jake's hand flew to his forehead. "Cher Horowitz. You're related to that lawyer Mel Horowitz! I've heard of him, of course, but didn't make the connection. I'm sorry." Gently, he covered my hand with his and ventured shyly, "Cher? Is there someplace we could just, you know, walk?"

I was taken aback. "Walk? You're in Beverly Hills, Jake. No one walks. That's practically a felony."

"Sorry." He shot me an imploring look and raked his fingers through his thick hair the same adorable way he'd done last night. "Look, I just think we can get to know each other better if I'm not having to deal with traffic, y'know?"

Briefly, I wondered if we couldn't get to know each other better in a trendy little bistro, but I let it go. And so, a little while later, I did something I'd never done before. And segue, for which I was so not wearing opportune footgear. In strappy platforms, I began to traipse the residential part of Rodeo Drive. We started at Sunset and headed south toward the boutique-driven Wilshire Boulevard.

Maybe it was the hiking element or just being with Jake, but somehow everything familiar felt different.

Like, I hadn't noticed it when we were driving? But it was such the smog-free, sun-dappled day. I turned my face up and let the rays caress my cheeks. And when you're driving, it's impossible to like, fall into step with someone. Sign: Jake and I took the exact same length strides.

Jake pointed up at the palm trees swaying gently in the afternoon breeze.

"Those trees are bizarre. So skinny with big leaves on top."

I giggled. "When I was little I used to think they looked like dancing telephone poles with fright wigs."

Jake laughed. "I know what you mean. They're lined up perfectly, just like the Radio City Rockettes—only wearing Don King wigs."

"The Radio City Rockettes?" I queried. "You mean, like in New York?"

For a sec Jake seemed uncomfortable. He mumbled, "I saw a picture of them once and that came to mind."

We were passing a righteous white stucco house that stood behind wrought-iron gates. "That's where Bruce Springsteen lived when he first moved to Beverly Hills. You know, in his model-slash-actress Julianne Phillips period."

Jake was fascinated. "Really? You're kidding! This must have been where he wrote 'Brilliant Disguise.' Oh, man, that song is amazing. Don't you think?"

I didn't. Think, that is. I hardly ever retain lyrics. And segue, my Springsteen expertise is pretty much limited to his social life and fashion sense: neither of which is remarkable. Still, if Jake had been any other boy, I would have A) changed the subject to one I do know something about, or B) faked it. I chose none of the above. I admitted ignorance. Which didn't bother Jake at all.

He explained. " 'Brilliant Disguise' is about how the face we put on for the world is a mask for who we really are. The singer can't tell what his girl's true feelings are—and conversely, he questions if he's showing his true soul to her."

That was intense! And wholly relatable. "I know what you mean, Jake. Like sometimes I'll put on glitter makeup and go to some festive charity soiree with Daddy. And all the guests will think, Isn't she jovial? Except, deep down, I'm stressing about Daddy scarfing cholesterol-addled hors d'oeuvres."

"That's it, uh, exactly." He paused. "And sometimes I come off more self-confident than I really am. When just beneath the surface, I'm a bundle of nerves."

"Like now?" I whispered, turning to him.

Jake took a deep breath and blushed slightly. "Yeah, like now. You have no idea."

Wordlessly, I slipped my hand into his and gave it a squeeze. He returned the gesture and then sheepishly admitted, "I'm not really into Springsteen. Except for that song. But I rule when it comes to the Beach Boys. I challenge anyone to beat my collection."

"Not so fast," I countered excitedly. Now here were stars I knew something about. "I bet you don't have the Pet Sounds album."

"You lose, Cher," he said with a huge grin—and then started singing the title song.

I burst out laughing. Jake's voice was horrible! "Don't quit your, uh, day job. I mean, school!"

He tilted his head and grinned. "Just making a point. Okay—name your Beach Boys albums. In order of favoriteness. Include all solo efforts."

"Hello, I'll even include all Wilson-Phillips off-shoots." As I ran down my collection—and okay, matched Jake in off-key singing, verse for verse—I radiated with joy. We were so on the same wave! Not just in our tandem taste for classic composers who double as American pop icons, either. We were both into No Doubt; we passionately believed Barenaked Ladies was underrated; Jamiroquai, overshticked—like what is with that Dr. Seuss hat?—and, in general, pop music suffers from Puff Daddy overload.

"And hello—Jewel!" I shook my head. "I allow some songs are deep, but her whole persona is faux. Like the transparent sheath she wore at the Grammys."

Jake vehemently agreed. "The wonder of the tundra. She puts on this whole *Julie of the Wolves,* I-grew-up-in-Alaska-and-lived-in-a-van thing, when all you have to do is dig a little deeper and the truth comes out. She went to Interlochen, that elite, artsy college in Michigan."

I got it. " 'Brilliant Disguise,' right?"

Jake tilted his head. "The song is universal, see?"

We were so passionately embroiled in our conversation, we barely noticed the car that was like, shadowing us. And, hello, I might not have noticed at all until I heard the distinct and distinctly annoying half-cackle, half-clucking of Amber Marins in her Jag. I spun around. Amber tilted her head and put a forefinger to her blush-overloaded cheek.

Clucking, she mused, "Cher walking. Cher with a date. So that must mean . . . Ginger Spice is First Lady."

I rolled my eyes. "Which would be preferable to an interface with you."

Amber gave me a sidelong glance of admonishment. "Tsk, tsk, Cher. Now where did you leave your manners? In your car, maybe?"

I sighed. Amber, the princess of obvious, was begging for an introduction. I caved. "Jake, I'd like you to meet—well, I wouldn't *like* it, exactly, but it seems out of my control at this point. This is Amber. An associate. From school."

Jake gamely reached out to shake Amber's hand. "I'm Jake Forrest. A, well, I guess, a friend of Cher's."

"Not." Amber threw her Jag into park and gripped Jake's hand. "I *know* every *friend* of Cher's, and believe me, Jake Forrest, I'd know if I knew you."

"Okay"—Jake grinned, expertly retracting his hand—"a recent friend. We sort of ran into each other for the first time last night."

Amber was puzzled. "Oh, so is this a first date kind of thing? How jocose. Is that why you're walking?" She paused a beat. "Why *are* you walking?"

I didn't want to waste valuable Jake-time explaining to Amber about the his-car-hitting-my-car thing. And about how our on-foot experience was massively exhilarating—until she showed up, that is. So I breezily quipped, "Hadn't you better be jetting off, Amber?

The sale at the reconstructive surgery boutique is almost over, and they're running out of your nose."

Amber was unfazed by my diss, but she did get the message. She waved and jauntily said, "Hope to see you again, Jake." Then she put platform to the pedal and darted back into the road, cutting off a Lexus and a Mercedes.

By the time I explained Amber to Jake—and told him about the rest of my friends—we'd reached Santa Monica Boulevard, the dividing line between über-wealthy houses and mega-expensive boutiques, boîtes, and bistros. But Jake, such the nonconformist, pointed to a Starbucks. "Up for a latte?"

Hello, I was up for an entire lunch. Preferably in some upscale trenderie, such as Barney Greengrass or the food emporium at the Tommy Hilfiger flagship store. Even Johnny Rockets would do.

But this was a day for firsts. I'd gone to a car body shop. And I'd walked. Lunch at Starbucks could be another pioneering experience.

I didn't regret it. Because it was there, while we waited on this like, endless line to order, that Jake and I so made the connection. It was furiously uncanny. We both decided on double-decaf, low-fat, light-froth lattes and veggie pita-roll sandwiches. We vehemently agreed on all vital topics, from music to movies— where our top ten lists coordinated like our outfits—to TV sitcoms, computer games, and books on required reading lists. In that category we gave *A Separate Peace* two thumbs up and agreed that *Jude the Obscure* should have stayed that way.

Jake mused, "When I was in high school, we

discussed that book for a month. God, I hated it. I kept falling asleep over it."

"Me, too! I always thought the Insomniacs Anonymous club should use it."

When our lattes and sandwiches were ready, I went to search out a table while Jake paid. He attempted to, anyway. The waitress seemed to have some issues with Jake's credit card. As in: she brutally cut it up, pronouncing it "Invalid!"

I'd just claimed our table when I rushed back over to the counter. Jake had turned Corvette red. He fished around for another card, mumbling, "Could I be more humiliated? I can't believe this is happening. Mom must have canceled the credit cards with the change of address."

Instantly I offered, "Forget it, Jake, no problem. I'll catch it." I whipped out my AmEx and handed it to the waitress. "Try this."

Jake's hand was shaking. "I feel like such a jerk. First the insurance thing, now this. You must think I'm pathetic."

I covered Jake's hand with mine. "Stop stressing. It's a major no big."

Hoping to spare Jake any more embarrassment, I gently guided him over to our table and steered the conversation away from credit-card chagrin. Since Jake had been reminiscing about his high school days, I went with, "So, what year are you in at UCLA?"

"What?" Jake was still mired in mortification. Gently, I repeated the question.

"UCLA, uh, right. I'm a sophomore. I started at San

Diego State and then transferred here. We decided to move here when I declared my major, which is a five-year program."

"What is it?"

"Law. Well, prelaw. I did a summer internship at a law firm back home, and that's when I decided on it. And that's why when you just told me whose daughter you were . . . well, Mel Horowitz is kind of legendary in legal circles."

The idea came upon me in waves. First a little lapping trickle. Then a more forceful, curlicued, white-capped splash. Then, finally, a surfworthy tsunami. Jake Forrest had proto-lawyer pedigree on par with Adam-not-the-gardener—hello, Jake attended the same school, had the same major, and had, even better, interned at an actual law firm. Jake could help Daddy research that heinous Heller case. And bonus, Daddy got me in the bargain! I could totally contribute. Daddy would get two for the price of one. How could he refuse?

Chapter 5

Daddy went adverbial. As in: Easily. Swiftly. Decisively. And addendum, majorly insensitively when he brutally rebuffed my brainstorm about Jake and me replacing Adam as research assistant in the all-consuming Heller case.

It was grossly unfair.

When I came home from my date with Jake, Daddy was alone in his study. Which I mistakenly took as a good sign.

Okay, maybe in retro? It *wasn't* the best time to approach the bench. But I could not contain myself. I was flying on the wings of soul mate ecstasy. Only Daddy was drowning in a sea of steely gray storage boxes, over which the top of his recently thinning hair poked. I made a mental note to start cataloging hair weaves, nutritional supplements, and products invented by Ron Popeil.

"Daddy," I began generically, but even so he tried to cut me off.

His "Not now, Cher" was accompanied by a dismissive wave of his hand and a firm "I need to focus on this."

I persevered. "That's just it, Daddy. I've come with the El Niño of focusing ideas." Before Daddy could shush me, I launched into a fully comprehensive explanation of how Jake and I could, nay, *should,* be the team on *his* team. How he'd get two for the price of one. "It's such the no-brainer, Daddy. We're ready to start now."

Okay, so grievously? If my paternal unit were to change career directions and enter the crowded rap star field? He could call himself Gruff Daddy. Because his entire reaction to my compelling argument was to growl, "Give it up, Cher! I don't have time for this now. You have no idea how critical this case is. Adam has already started. I can't change course in midstream."

"Can't or won't?" I don't usually do petulant—the lower lip protrusion thing always trashes my lipliner—but Daddy's mulish response triggered my juvenile one.

After that it was way domino—as in effect, not the all-hours pizza delivery—the way *my* petulant set off *his* postal. He totally thundered, "Cher, that's enough! I don't want your help on this case! I don't need your constant interruptions when I'm working! What part of 'no' don't you understand?"

My lip trembled. My liner and my gloss were goners. The stinging sensation in my eyes signaled imminent mascara migration. I briefly considered the effect a sob-fest would have on Daddy: he'd either cave or go completely atomic. I couldn't risk further alienation, so I turned on my chunky Aldo platforms and stomped upstairs.

I listened hard for Daddy's conciliatory "I'm sorry" trailing me. But only silence followed me up the stairs. I shattered it by slamming my door.

Okay, so like no maturity award for me. But today's emotional roller coaster—ecstasy with Jake, agony with Daddy—can so not be good for my psyche. Not to mention my skin. I spent the next hour moisturizing, revitalizing, and applying layers of herbal facial mask to my cheeks, nose, and forehead.

And being on the phone. At times like this, there is no substitute for t.b.'s.

I called De and did a post-date report. Recapping the salient points of the day took me over the moon again. "I'm kvelling for you, Cher," De squealed.

But then recapping my fractious interface with Daddy bummed me out all over again. On that count De urged a major time-out. "Then reapproach the bench, Cher. He's a lawyer. He's used to the appeals process. This time get your timing down better. The verdict will go in your favor."

I called Murray. The boy POV is furiously crucial in interpreting hidden signs on first dates. But Murray was little help. "I gotta meet the dude, Cher. I can't interpret anything without an up-close. He could come off like a lean, mean soul mate machine to you, but *I* gotta look him in the eye. Then I'll know."

I called Sean. But instead of offering advice, girlfriend-challenged Sean requested some. His latest crush, Kristen-Megan-Nicole—her parents had gotten stuck in the trendy-name ambivalent zone—remained oblivious to him. "What should I do, Cher? I've tried everything. Calling. E-mailing. Notes in her locker. I even applied to join some club she's in, Los Picaros."

I suggested Sean might want to actually *take* Spanish before applying for enrollment in the Spanish club, Los Picaros. Then I gave him Madame Tiara's hot line number.

I considered calling Amber, high priestess of parental manipulation. But one Amber encounter a day was enough.

So I called Jake. Back in Starbucks, I'd explained all about Daddy and his frantic cry for help on the Heller case. Jake had gone spongy, absorbing every detail. He'd been way flattered at my suggestion that we pitch in. So it hurt to have to tell him about Daddy's brutal rebuff.

Jake's voice betrayed his bummed feelings, but he reacted way rationally. And bonus, he exhibited intense philosophical understanding.

"I know you're disappointed, Cher. I am, too. I was looking forward to helping your dad, especially since it meant getting to spend more time with you. But he said no, and we probably shouldn't push it."

"But I really want to help," I protested. "And besides, I want you to meet Daddy. When he's more himself."

Jake paused. "And when he doesn't think I'm just this hit-and-run driver without insurance, right?"

"Not even!" I started to contradict, but deep down I knew Jake was right. Temporarily. Once Daddy met him, he'd see the truth.

Jake continued. "Maybe together you and I can figure out a way to help your dad that isn't against his wishes. Let's give it time, get stuff settled, and then put our heads together. I bet between the two of us, we can come up with something."

Jake's use of the phrases "put our heads together" and "between the two of us" rocked my world.

So did his answer when I finally got the courage to ask him. Jake was an Aries.

Still, I tossed and turned all that night, furiously wrinkling my Lauren sheet set. I was stuck in a quagmire of contradictory feelings. Jake Forrest—the sweet, adorable, understanding, studmuffin of my dreams—had arrived in my life. I should have been floating on low-smog-alert air.

But how could I float, even with water wings, when Daddy's harsh had stung me so? His stubborn rebuke dragged me down into the depths of like, the subbasement at Neiman's, where sale items like housecoats and hammers live.

It was only through visualizing techniques that I was able to sleep at all.

But by the next morning, I'd made a decision. I

opted to go with De's suggestion of an appeal, delayed by a time-out. That would give Daddy time to defrost and see my floodlight suggestion for the brilliance it was.

It would have worked, too, only tragically? I barely saw Daddy over the entire next week. During my time-out, Daddy flew out. Literally.

On Sunday, over a virtuous brunch of grapefruit halves, egg-white omelettes, and herbal tea, Daddy delivered his upcoming schedule to me. Because the Heller case wasn't the only one on his docket, his presence was required in far-flung zip codes. That very night he was booked on the red-eye to New York for a Monday meeting. From there it was on to Chicago and then to Dallas. Or Denver. Or Detroit. One of those *D* cities the Weather Channel obsesses about.

Upshot? Daddy would be ghost, like all week.

Worse, he had no intention of revisiting his decision on my offer to help.

After brunch Daddy furiously paced the length and breadth of our family-slash-media room. While the aerobic benefits of furious pacing are noteworthy, Daddy's angst counteracted them. His business trip had come up suddenly and he "wasn't comfortable" with the idea of me staying alone all week. He wanted to ask our most amenable relative, Grandma Ray, to come stay with me. She's Mom's mom and lives in a condo in Santa Monica. When I was younger, she often stayed with me when Daddy was away.

But now? Not even.

I didn't want to make Daddy go postal again, so I

displayed admirable maturity. "I understand your discomfort, Daddy. If I were a parent, I'd feel such the same way. Potentially. And segue, I'm rampantly devoted to Grandma, but, hello, I'm seventeen. In some states that makes me old enough to have children who can stay home alone."

Tragically, Daddy had zoned out. His next suggestion, if possible, was further down the humiliation scale. He actually stroked his chin, musing, "You know, Adam has to be here anyway, working in my study. And he's a good kid. He's got street sense. Maybe I'll ask him to move in for a few days."

I fell out of the maturity zone, screeching, "To what, baby-sit me?"

Before Daddy could respond, two things happened. Daddy's business line rang and so did my cellular. Daddy dismissed me with a "We'll continue this discussion later" and went to take his call.

De was on my line. I'd nearly forgotten that my main big and I had made a phone date to do tandem calculus homework and then review the tape of the VH-1 Fashion Awards. We needed to rewind and pause several times before coming down with our final pronouncements. Like, Fiona Apple: savant seer or whiny brat? What *is* her childhood issue? And how does it affect her fashion sense? Such multitasking took up my entire afternoon.

But I couldn't let Daddy leave with unresolved feelings; we needed closure. So by dinner that night, we hammered out a compromise. It was like Grandma's favorite old PBS series, *Upside/Downside*. He agreed—like, chuh!—that I didn't need a baby-sitter. And due to his physical absence, he lifted the ban on my credit card spending. But he stood firm on his rebuff of my help on the Heller case. And he still totally did not want to know about Jake. Anything, except: "His insurance company better have settled with ours by the time I get back."

Before the airport limo arrived, I tiptoed into his study and planted a kiss on his stubbly cheek. "Get some sleep on the plane, Daddy," I counseled sagely. "I packed some tangerine therapy aftershave in your suitcase. Use it, okay?"

Daddy gazed at me with weary eyes. "Be sure the house alarm is on, Cher. And no going out on a school night. And call Grandma if you want company. Or—"

Before he could say "Adam," I assured him I'd be fine. I was committed to following the rules. And, hello, he knew where he could beep me. He said he would, frequently.

Because I was car- and Daddy-devoid, De and Murray rotated taking me to school for the week. Not that it's out of their way.

We're all juniors at Bronson Alcott High, a public school with private school sensibilities and amenities. Like latte machines and juice bars in the hallways, valet parking, and by calling 777-TUSH, reserved seating in the auditorium. Bronson Alcott offers classes in all basic subjects, reworked to fit our cutting-edge lifestyle. Like, geometry is called Touched by an Angle. American person-story is compulsory for sophomores, and the class formerly known as geography has been retitled How I Spent My Summer Vacation.

We have a choice of science, or sci-fience, sometimes taught by visiting professor David Duchovny. We offer zip-code appropriate electives, such as water polo, polo ponies, Polo by Lauren, and our most popular elective, surgery.

Our school provides an aesthetically appropriate environment for outdoor dining and pre-homeroom flaunting. That would be the Quad, our lavishly landscaped faux piazza. Bordered by palm and eucalyptus trees, ringed with a jogging trail, it's dotted with marble benches, potted azalea bushes, and Evianspouting wishing fountains into which expired and/or maxed-out credit cards are tossed by the despondent. Everyone hangs in the Quad.

At school De and I are undisputed leaders, a position we take very seriously. We're so popular that when we posed for our own milk mustache poster, the cafeteria sales of skim, 2%, and even homogenized rivaled *Scream 2*'s opening weekend. The Lactose Intolerant Club demanded equal time for soy mustache posters.

This Monday morning no lactose lined my lip. As my friends listened intently, all I could talk about was Jake. "He's the total package, everything Madame Tiara said my soul mate would be. He's highly evolved. Intelligent. Philosophical. Idealistic. A hottie to die for."

Murray, his arm possessively around De, commented, "I'll reserve judgment until I meet him. But personally? I'm down with that horror-scope stuff. 'Cause I'm De's soul mate, right, baby? Admit it. Am I not the most intelligent, idealistic, evolved man of your dreams?"

De tossed her classically coiffed mane and narrowed her long-lashed eyes. "You forgot the most salient point. You know you're lucky to have me."

"That too, baby," Murray agreed, nuzzling De's nose.

Sean, taking in the touching scene, wistfully eyed Kristen-Megan-Nicole, who'd just strolled by, one of a gaggle of girlfriends. "That does it, I'm calling that Madame Tiara hot line number. If she's my soul mate, I have to know."

I squeezed Sean's elbow. "I so agree. I don't know if Kristen-Megan-Nicole is your twin soul, but I know there's someone out there for you. Just like Jake was out there for me. And now he's here in my life. He's perfect."

"Excuse me, Kathie Lee. No one is perfect. Not without surgical intervention." Amber, the fashion slayer, had arrived. And it was all open mouth, insert open-toed shoe.

I trounced. "Point taken, Ambu-liposuction. But who would know better than you? Alas, so much surgical perfection oft goes awry. I cite: Tori Spelling. And you."

But Amber had latched onto something and like yet another season of *Baywatch*, droned on. "So, about your first date with Mr. Perfect. What's the deal with the walking thing, Cher? I mean, excuse me for remarking on your downward mobility, but doesn't he have a car?"

Before I could retort, Amber pounced. "And I *know* where you had lunch last Saturday, so don't even think about issuing a denial. My spies are everywhere."

At that, De, Murray, and Sean eyeballed me suspiciously. Amid all my post-date reports, I did sort of omit a few of the less enchanting details.

Amber, owner of exclusive gossip, licked her chops. "So, about lunch. Did Mr. Perfect Soul Mate spring for someplace special? Or especially ubiquitous? He*llo*, Starbucks!"

De's hand flew to her throat. She gasped in horror.

Amber cracked witty. "Did I mention they're opening a branch . . . in my living room?"

Murray and Sean guffawed at Amber's quip. "Your living room! That's funn—"

Only De's sharp elbow to his ribs stopped Murray from giving further credence to Amber's highly evolved—not—wit.

In spite of her own pique at not knowing the walking and Starbucks parts, De rallied. "If Cher says he's her one and only, I believe her. I'm sure he had reasons for lunch at . . ."

De couldn't bring herself to say it, so she trailed off, "That . . . place."

Before Amber could heap another diss on me the bell rang, signaling homeroom was about to begin. Our posse strolled into the ivy-covered academic building together and settled into our seats in Mr. Mazza's homeroom class.

During attendance I announced, "I can't wait for my homies to meet Jake. Appointment books, everyone. We'll schedule a date. ASAP."

From our designer backpacks, slingbacks, and attaché cases, we accessed electronic organizers, laptops, and leather appointment books. I called Jake on my cellular, and together we tried to find a uni-convenient time.

Only, as anyone who's ever tried to schedule a group encounter knows, the frustration level is massive. Like Tom Cruise trying to see over Nicole Kidman's head.

All our schedules—including Jake's—were total gridlock alert. If *we* were free, *he* had a class. If *he* had a break, *we* had tennis, golf, or spinning classes, or someone's personal trainer just could not be rescheduled.

Whatever. Jake and I kept trying. We talked between all my classes. In the morning, he called to assure me the car insurance thing was being fully handled. Next period I called him back to assure him I knew he'd come through. During his lunch break, he put the phone to his CD player so I could hear "Brilliant Disguise." I shared an entire day's worth of observations with him.

In our last period class, When Chemicals Attack, he beeped me again. Jake whispered, "I just wanted to hear your voice."

I elbowed De, my lab partner at the Madame Curie memorial table. She was pouring some puce liquid from test tube to beaker in an attempt to discover next season's cutting-edge fashion hue. "Jake just wanted to hear my voice. How sweet is that?"

I expected De to totally coo. Only suddenly, her head jerked up. She pointed to a speaker mounted high on the wall and commanded, "Shh!"

I looked up. "What?"

"They're making an announcement. It's about the PSAT results."

Over the newly installed high-definition PA system, Principal Lehrer's voice furiously boomed. "Attention Bronson Alcott junior class. Because of the zip drive computerized system we donated to the Educational Testing Center, our PSAT results are being rush-released. They'll be announced tomorrow."

A gargantuan gasp reverberated through all junior classrooms. Snippets of horrified reactions bounced off the walls. "As in tomorrow, the day after today? *That* tomorrow? How could they do that? They didn't factor in prep time! What speech-writer can I get on such short notice?"

The terror was understandable. In our first year here, De and I started the Bronson Alcott tradition of dressing up and preparing acceptance speeches for Test Result Day. Be it midterms, finals, tardy awards, cheerleading contests, or any standardized tests, we pioneered the concept of meeting our fates fashionably and articulately. Our theory: high school is supposed to prepare us for life. Statistically, our peer group will be attending more vote-driven events than any other. Who among us will not one day attend the Oscars, Emmys, Grammys, Golden Globes, and even Blockbuster Awards? It's never too early to practice proper style.

So, like, wasn't it ironic, I warbled, as Murray drove me home that afternoon. A few days ago, I would have been as wigged as my buds at the Test Result Day time-challenge. But now that Jake was in my life, everything seemed doable. And I would have joined De, Murray, Sean, and Amber on their emergency mall troll, but on the ride home, Jake called—he'd snagged tickets to the Tibetan Freedom concert tonight.

Could we not go? Jake was majorly, passionately devoted to supporting human rights. Making the world a better place. Just like me. He'd be picking me up at seven.

Chapter 6

After I clicked off the phone, the wheels in my brain began to spin like a dreidel at Hanukkah. A concert date with Jake tonight! A concert for a global cause! What would I wear? Would other well-known supporters like Brad Pitt be there? Richard Gere? Cindy Crawford? Or had she forfeited custody of the cause when the marriage imploded? I was pondering those vital issues when Murray dropped me off at home. I barely noticed Adam's putt-putt car chugging into the driveway behind us.

But when apple-cheeked Adam emerged, I couldn't squash the tide of ill will that engulfed me. Nor the snipe at his vehicle.

"Cute car. Isn't that Motor Trend of the Year's Award Winner—for 1972?"

Adam glanced at Murray's Beemer as it pulled out of the driveway. He shifted his tattered briefcase from under his left arm to his right and shrugged. "What can I say, Cher? Not everyone can afford to be a slave to the trendmobile market."

Turning away from him, I pulled the house keys out of my Tignanello slingback. "So what are you implying, Adam? That my friends are superficial? And by association, so am I?"

"If the high heel fits . . ."

I opened the front door and rolled my eyes. "For one thing, the expression *high heels* went out with the era of your car. They're platforms. And for another, hello, what gives you the right to judge the character of the driver by the car he or she drives?"

Adam followed me in the house. "I don't. But isn't that the golden rule you live—or at least choose your dates—by?"

"That is so casting aspersions." I began to fume, although Adam wasn't categorically wrong. I spun around to face him. "You, of course, are above making assumptions about people."

"I try to be a little more evolved than that," he said evenly, lifting his chin.

"Yet the first time you walked into our house, you assumed that just because I'm female, I cooked dinner. How evolved is that?" I so nailed him.

"Touché, Cher, but so was your assumption that just because I buy my clothes at Old Navy, I must be the gardener."

"As if! I misheard Daddy's introduction."

"You misheard it because your assumption, based on my appearance, was already made."

"Whatever, Adam. Think what you want. But you're wrong. Mostly."

"Well, Cher, much as I'd like to continue this interlude, the meter is ticking."

I was confused. "There's a taxi outside? But your car . . ."

Adam shook his head. "It's an expression. It means time is money. Your dad's paying me to be here, and I refuse to waste his time or his money."

"Daddy's paying you?" I couldn't disguise my surprise. Most UCLA prelaw grunts beg to work here just for the prestige of a Mel Horowitz & Associates notation on their résumés. That, plus they get school credit.

As if Adam could read my mind, he explained dourly, "Unlike most of the people in your limited orbit, I'm not in the position to work for free. I actually need the money."

I was livid—and thoughtful. I went all Ally McBeal. What I thought was, Adam must be a major legal brain for Daddy to choose him over someone who would work for free. But like I'd give Adam the satisfaction of a compliment? Not even. So what I said was, "You don't even know me, Adam. Or my orbit."

He cleared his throat. "I'm taking an educated guess here. Who do you even know that has *one* job—let alone two?"

"You have two jobs?"

Adam nodded his head and then strode into Daddy's study. Over his shoulder, he replied, "I tutor part-time."

I paused by the portrait of Mom on my way upstairs to get ready for my Tibetan Freedom date with Jake. "So what do you think, Mom? How can I get Daddy to see that choosing Adam over me is a grievous goof?"

Mom considered. I couldn't interpret her answer. But when I asked, "Okay, about tonight: trousers, skirt, or dress? Tube top, camisole, or chenille mock turtle?" Mom's concerned visage reminded me that the concert might be outdoors. Layers was the answer.

As it so often is.

Even though she's dead, Mom knows best. Several hours later, huddled next to Jake on an unseasonably blustery LA night, I gave silent thanks for her sage advice. The concert, massively crowd-driven, was in an outdoor stadium. Tragically, our seats were row NC— Nosebleed City; Section S—as in Siberia.

Jake, studly in a Nautica jacket, wasn't bugged by the wind or the altitude. When I noted that all I could see of Alanis were her severely untamed split ends, Jake shrugged. His eyes danced. "I'm just so psyched to be here—with you!—I don't care where we sit. Besides, how lucky could we get—snagging tickets at the last minute?"

I fished for my ticket, which I'd stuffed inside my pocket. My second keepsake forever souvenir from Jake. I took it out and gave it a little kiss. I was about to stuff it back in my pocket when I happened to eyeball the back of it. The word "Complimentary" was stamped across it.

"Free seats?" I was surprised.

"I got them from a guy at school," Jake explained less sheepishly than he might have.

"But isn't this concert supposed to be raising money for a worthy cause?"

"It doesn't get more worthy, Cher," Jake responded, craning his neck to see the next act, the Mighty Mighty Bosstones.

I persisted. "But wouldn't getting in free defeat the purpose? How exactly did we contribute to the cause, if not financially?"

Jake quickly turned to me. Tenderly he cupped my chin. "It's the show of support, Cher. Money isn't everything. Life isn't only about that. C'mere."

I scooched over closer to him. His aura was massively masculine, like a Polo cologne sniff strip in *Details*. "Like, duh, Jake. I'm aware. And I know that Tibet is a beautiful, sacred place we should protect. Standing up for human rights is seriously proper. Yet it has been my experience that all righteous causes have expenses and——"

The Santa Ana winds were playing massive havoc with my hair. Gently, Jake brushed a stray strand off my face. "I know all about Tibet," he said. "That's why we're here. What I don't know a lot about is you. Talk to me, Cher."

I did. But it was whenever I mentioned Daddy that Jake went all follow-up. All during the Bosstones set he totally peppered me with questions about Daddy's cases. I told him everything I knew. And then it dawned on me: Jake *worships* litigation legend Mel Horowitz.

Which made me feel all the more bummed at Daddy's steadfast refusal to allow us to help out. And, mental note, all the more determined to find a way around that.

I was in the middle of relating the details of one of Daddy's most heinous tax evasion cases when the newly anointed kings of hip, Radiohead, barreled onstage. The screams of the SRO audience drowned out our conversation. And then when the Beastie Boys totally came out of retirement to free Tibet, the noise level intensified.

In fact, if my beeper hadn't been the vibrating kind, I might not have noticed it going off at all. I checked the readout, expecting De or Amber even. So when a New York area code showed up, I was startled. Momentarily.

Startled turned to panic: Daddy! He must have tried calling me at home and gotten my voice mail. Which meant he'd surmised the truth: that "no going out on a school night when I'm out of town" edict? I'd spaced. Like, serious oops.

I had a decision to make. Whip out my cellular and call him back? Or not. Just pretend, what, I was in the bath when he called? Return the call when I got home? But I couldn't delay. What if Daddy needed me? What if Pater wasn't merely checking up?

Excusing myself, I dashed to the ladies' room and called the number on the digital readout.

"Hi, Daddy," I said cheerily after the hotel operator connected me to his room. "Greetings from the Big Orange! How goes it in the Big Apple?"

Daddy wasn't in the mood for a citrus comparison—especially since it was like, close to midnight where he was. "Why aren't you home, Cher? Where are you?" he demanded testily.

Stalling for time, I repeated, "Where am I?" I looked around. Just then a Betty in a bone Prada suit strutted by. "I'm . . . I'm . . . at the mall. Getting an emergency outfit for tomorrow when they announce PSAT results."

I told a fib that would have been the truth had I not been freeing Tibet. Or something. Whatever. Daddy wasn't thrilled—but he wasn't as postal as he would have been had he known the actual truth. In all? A bullet dodged.

Like, major whew!

The next day I felt like I'd walked into a dream. Correction: a nightmare. The one where like, everyone knows something you don't. The dream where you forgot your homework/didn't prepare for a test/came to school undressed. Tragically, this was no dream. This was real.

The entire Bronson Alcott junior class had gone designer garb overboard for Test Result Day. Except me. I'd been freeing Tibet. With Jake. And, addendum, expertly circumventing Daddy's long-distance postal.

None of which made me feel any better when I strode into the Quad. I felt like Janeane Garofalo at the Oscars. Except I wasn't trying to make a counter-culture statement by wearing a T-shirt. I'd just forgotten the significance of the day. I'd done Abercrombie & Fitch instead of Dolce & Gabbana. As De would say? "Oy vey."

The first to pounce on me—like, doy—was Amber. Draped in an ensemble from her Insane Clown Posse couture collection, she went all Joan Rivers, shoving a microphone in my face.

"And who do we have here?" Amber dragged me up to a hastily constructed stage area. Commanding her fashion-cam crew to focus on me, she announced, "Why, if it isn't Cher Horowitz! Everyone! Look—Cher has arrived!"

I smiled and, mainly out of habit, waved to my schoolmate admirers. They all—to a worshipper—went slack-jawed at my fashion crash.

Amber cattily purred, "And what exact design statement are we making today, Cher? That you couldn't think of what to wear on such a critically important day? That you are not—as in, never were and never will be—Bronson Alcott's fashion leader? That you relinquish your popularity crown to moi?"

Before Amber could shove me any further down the humiliation slide, De and Murray flew up to the stage and hustled me off. "No statements," De said angrily as Murray covered the fashion-cam lens with his hand. "She has no comment."

My main and her boo had done a Will and Jada matching thing. They were both in shades of sorbet, the hue du moment. Sean stuck with citrus: tried and true to his vitamin-enriched personality.

The three of them formed a human wall around me and spirited me into the recently upgraded Sherry Lansing Auditorium. De whispered, "What's going on, Cher? Why didn't you dress? Why didn't you call me back last night? I could have used your help writing my acceptance speech. I left six messages on your machine."

Sheepishly, I admitted, "I was with Jake last night. Supporting Tibetan freedom. I got home way late. And then . . . I'm sorry, De, I just forgot."

De stopped in her tracks. She shot Murray and Sean an uh-oh look. Translation: Cher's lost it. She's allowed a mere boy to make her forget about fashion. She's risked her popularity and status at school—over a boy.

I would have hung my head in shame. But what they still failed to realize? Jake wasn't just any boy. He was my soul mate, my other half. I think.

Serendipitously, the Test Result Day announcements were about to begin. The auditorium was filled to capacity, not just with juniors. The entire school attended. De and Amber snagged aisle seats. That way, when their names were announced as Top Scorers, Math and Verbal, they'd be spared the klutziness of tripping over anyone to stride up to the stage to make their acceptance speeches.

Except that he was neither amusing nor clever and hadn't prepared an opening medley, Principal Lehrer was the Billy Crystal of the event. Of course, our principal didn't bear responsibility for *City Slickers II*, either. Whatever. He did get the ball rolling quickly.

"To present our first award," the principal announced, "I give you Bronson Alcott's thoroughly tenured twosome, Coach Diemer and Mr. Mazza."

Our tall, buff homeroom/guidance teacher with our stocky yet muscular PE coach? Such the daring pairing! Dressed in teacher togs, they traded a few hastily composed quasi-lame quips and then announced the nominees for Best Penmanship in the PSATs.

Okay, so that's not one of the categories other schools might recognize. But, hello, did I not mention how advanced Bronson Alcott is? We wholly subscribe to the mid- to late-'90s "everyone is gifted" concept. Our theory is that each student should be nominated for something. After all, don't our idols always tell us what an honor it is just to be nominated? It's a self-esteem enhancer.

So for the next three hours—although our Test Result Day Awards always run long—we sat at the edge of our seats and rooted for our favorites. Their names were sporadically butchered by nearsighted teachers unused to working with a TelePrompTer.

The Doogie Howser Penmanship award, also known as Best Filling in of the Ovals, went to last year's class president, Brian Fuller. He totally credited his number-two pencils. And his parents, of course. He marched offstage happily pressing his Cottie—that's what our award is called—to his chest.

Best Dressed Male on PSAT Day went to one of our crowd: Murray! We robustly chanted, "Go, Murray! Go, Murray!" as he proudly sauntered up to accept. Naturally, Murray thanked his parents for their financial contribution to his wardrobe. But his most sincere thank-you went to, "My woman, Dionne. She shopped, she schlepped, she selected my entire outfit for that day."

De kvelled! She also scribbled down a note to thank Murray when it was her turn to take the stage.

Best Dressed Female—the one I usually take—went this year to Annabelle Gurwich. Yet I felt no outrage. It was A) an honor to be nominated in such stellar company, and B) I knew that this was probably the only award Annabelle would get. While I was sure to snag Best Tressed.

Surprisingly? I didn't. Of the five nominees, including Amber—though her real hair hasn't even cameoed all semester—the award was given to our Betty of the buzz cut, Baez. And yet, I was bummed devoid. Minor affronts like these faded next to my new relationship with Jake.

There were awards given for Finished First, Finished Last, and even one for the student who'd finished on the dot of the halfway point.

The Bill Gates Award for Potential Unrecognized Genius—formerly known as Needs the Most Improvement—went to Sean. Again our clique applauded wildly. I totally thumbs-upped when Sean took his moment in the spotlight to thank Kristen-Megan-Nicole. "If she hadn't ignored me all semester, I might have been able to concentrate. And then I would never have earned this award."

Finally, they were ready to announce two biggies: Top Scorer in Math and Top Scorer in Verbal. Traditionally, math came first. De smoothed her Versace shift, so it wouldn't wrinkle when she got up. Mrs. DeMicco, our sci-fience teacher, beamed. "The envelope, please."

All eyes in the auditorium were riveted on De. I was flushed with excitement for my t.b. I winked and squeezed her hand.

"And this year's Top Scorer in Math is . . ."

De gripped the armrests of her seat and started to propel herself up.

Which is the position she froze in—sort of half up and half not—when Mrs. DeMicco announced . . .

"Cher Horowitz!"

A collective gasp filled the auditorium—the loudest was mine. How could that be? I mean, I'm a dependable ninety-ninth percentiler, but to top De? Not even.

Sean pulled me out of my stunned. "Get up," he urged. "You're making it worse by just sitting there. Go get your award."

I turned to De. Her face was stony. She attempted to smile supportively, but she knew and I knew, her face would have cracked. I whispered, "We'll demand a recount. This belongs to you."

On wholly wobbly legs, I got up to accept. Onstage, I whispered to Principal Lehrer, "There must be some mistake. Are you sure?"

He insisted, "Zip drives don't lie."

Underdressed and unprepared, I faced the audience. I winged it. I tried to make light. I thanked De for making "that one goof." No one laughed. No one cheered. No one chanted, "Go, Cher!"

I felt deeply undeserving. Like a Spice Girl at the Grammys.

Clutching my Cottie, I returned to my seat. Finally, it was time to move on to the last award.

Coach Diemer did the honors. "And this year's Bronson Alcott Top Scorer in Verbal—Reading Comprehension and Vocabulary—is . . ."

Amber's hand shot up. "Wait!" she commanded. "Lip liner 911! Do not announce my name yet." She whipped out a compact and lined her lips, while everyone waited. I couldn't even react to her gall. Like, whatever. Let's get this over with so I can make reparations to De.

I was fully invested in pondering how I would do that. So I was like, the only one who didn't hear it the first time, but only on video playback: "Ladies and gentlemen, for the first time in Bronson Alcott history we have a grand-slammer. Our Top Scorer, Verbal, is, once again, CHER HOROWITZ!"

The silence was deafening. Like Pamela Anderson playing *Jeopardy!* It was only when Amber bumped her head into the chair in front of her that anyone moved. She'd passed out.

It's like that famous poem about a tree falling in the forest. Like if no one hears it, did it really fall? Or something. With my history-making Top Scorer in Math and in Verbal on the PSATs, if I had no one to celebrate with—did it really count? Or something.

Tragically, my t.b.'s were too shell-shocked—not to mention wigged out—to share the moment. De was fully in a daze. She never heard me trying to apologize. Murray, out of loyalty to De, couldn't bring himself to give me even one snap. Sean, out of loyalty to Murray, shrugged and explained that his whole friendship was at stake. He was congratulations ambivalent.

Amber revived only long enough to stalk away, glaring. For once, her verbal veracity failed her.

I felt totally uncomfortable. Like Mariah Carey might in an ensemble that covers her skin. I'd just made high school history—I should have been profoundly pumped. My t.b.'s should have been giving me serious props. Instead, they were treating me like such the pariah.

I called Jake. Sensing my angst, he offered to ditch his afternoon classes to be with me. But how could I let him do that? I took a taxi home.

When I got back, the house was empty. Like my PSAT victory. I might have taken a slide down to pity city, but as I flopped on my queen-size, Jake called again. Tenderly, he was all, "You sound like you really need a friend, Cher. What about if I come over later, maybe around dinner?"

I was suddenly struck with inspiration.

"Bring your bathing suit," I advised him as visions of a moonlight swim in our backyard pool danced in my head.

By the time we hung up, my spirits were on the upswing. I left an apologetic message for De, feeling secure that given time, she'd get over her disappointment. Like maybe the zip drive did screw up. Whatever.

I called Indochine, a total temple of Asian eats, first making sure that this cuisine didn't contribute to the occupation of Tibet. I ordered the Romantic Peking Duck for two. It came with candles, pot stickers, and all appropriate water-fowl accessories.

Then I ran a hot, steamy shower and changed into a soul-mate-coming-to-dinner appropriate outfit: Max Mara drawstring pants and Sigrid Olsen mockneck top. I took extra time on my hair. I'd seen this slammin' 'do in the latest *Allure,* brushed back in front and twisty braid in the back. It gave me a look that screamed, "sleek and haphazard." It was also water-worthy.

When the bell rang a few minutes later, I assumed dinner was being delivered. So, makeup-challenged, I trundled down the stairs. But when I flung open our etched-glass double doors, there stood Jake. He looked hot. Over his shoulder was an athletic bag. In his hands, two glorious sunflowers.

"For the Top Scorer in Math. And the Top Scorer in Verbal. I'm so proud of you, Cher!" His eyes twinkled as he handed them to me.

My heart sang. Someone appreciated my accomplishment. Could he not be my intellectual match? My twin soul?

"Make yourself at home, Jake," I ordered, pointing the way to the family room. "I just need to finish my makeup."

As I ran upstairs, Jake called out, "You look amazing just the way you are."

Without makeup? Not even. Still, knowing he thought so, I did an abridged version of cosmetic application. When I came back downstairs, Jake was staring at one of the paintings on the wall.

"Your house is amazing, Cher," he said admiringly. "I don't claim to be an expert, but isn't that a Monet?"

"Daddy has excellent taste," I murmured modestly.

Slowly, Jake walked around, cocking his head, studying the sculptures, the Etruscan era vases, complementing Daddy's totally tasteful modern and Jurassic art collection. He fully gasped at the portrait that hangs just by the bottom of our staircase. "Wow! What a beautiful woman." He whistled. "Who is she?"

Mom.

Okay, so like this relationship I have with Mom? It's so not something I randomly share. Like, talking to a painting of your deceased mother? How wiggy is that? Yet I knew Jake would understand. So, shyly, I told him. Not only who the painting was, but all about our relationship.

Jake took my hands in his. His cobalt eyes seared into mine. "I don't know what to say, Cher. That's so personal. I'm touched you shared that with me. And I want you to know, you can tell me anything."

I blushed wildly and went articulate-anemic. "It's just that . . . I don't know. From the moment we met, it's like . . . I felt there was something different about you. Special, somehow."

Jake proved me right by sharing *his* most personal secret. He told me about his dad. About how they used to be so close—like Tiger and Earl Woods, except without the golf. But then some heinous incident happened, and his dad, well, didn't live with them anymore.

Gently I tried to probe further, but it was too painful for Jake to continue. I understood. I could wait.

And then? Jake gently wrapped his arms around me and pulled me close. I lifted my chin. I closed my eyes. I fully expected the next sensation I would feel would be his soft, full lips brushing mine. So like, imagine my chagrin when instead, I felt the jarring vibrations of the front door slamming.

I jumped. Jake dropped his arms from around me.

And the Bad Timing of the Century award goes to . . . Adam!

He totally charged through the foyer, on his way to Daddy's study. When he saw me and Jake at the bottom of the stairs, he did a double-take. "Oh . . . Cher! Sorry, I didn't know you were here. Your car wasn't in the driveway."

"Well, duh, Adam, that's because it's in the repair shop."

He glanced at Jake. "Right. I knew that. I guess I missed your car. Look, I didn't mean to disturb you kids. I'll just head into Mel's study and get to work."

Adam started to lope off in that direction, but I grabbed his elbow. He swung around to face me. Fuming at his "you kids" remark, I was about remind him like, whose house this was. Only I was viciously struck with the hue of his hazel eyes. It uncannily matched his hair. So what I said came out a little less buggin' than I'd meant it to.

"Adam, our front door locks automatically when you close it. And, adjunct, the alarm resets itself automatically. How did you get in?"

Adam adeptly released his elbow from my grip. "Mel gave me the key and the alarm code. Didn't he tell you?"

Chapter 7

*O*n an emotional scale, my day had been Space Mountain—up, down, and twisty, startling surprises around every corner. I should have figured my theme of a romantic evening with Jake would get derailed. Starting with: I had to introduce Jake to Adam, who still hadn't made it past us into Daddy's study.

Then my date, generous and inclusive, actually invited Adam to eat with us. The clue-challenged law student, oblivious to the pity invite, tragically accepted.

Good thing Indochine sends oversize portions. Expertly, I divided our romantic, candlelight dinner for two into three—which is, as opposed to the classic TV sitcom, *not* company.

Jake tried to make polite conversation about the Heller case, but Adam went all circumspect. Instead,

Adam went all need-to-knowy about Jake's professors and what courses he was taking, and then made this big deal that he'd never heard of the names Jake mentioned.

"It's a big school," Jake said, shrugging. He changed the subject. "Enough about us. This is Cher's day. A toast to Cher!" He raised his glass.

Adam, unaware that speaking while chewing signals a virulent strain of icky, stuffed a pot sticker into his mouth before asking, "Why's that?"

When Jake informed him of my PSAT coup, Adam nearly choked on his dumpling. All he could muster was, "You're kidding."

I drummed my French tips on the table. "Why, Adam? Do I not look like your idea of the academically enhanced? Are we judging by looks alone?"

Adam swallowed and tried to cover up his embarrassment. "It's just that . . . well, it's unusual for one person to ace both parts of the test. Most people excel in one area. It's a right brain/left brain thing."

I shot him a huge victory smile. "I'm good with coordinating. I was born with the mix-and-matching gene."

Adam blinked. "Well, I guess you won't be signing up for my tutoring course."

"Your what course?" I asked absently, intent on spearing a pot sticker before Adam ate them all.

"I run a PSAT tutoring course. Remember, my second job? UCLA tuition is a tough nut . . ." He trailed off, realizing Jake was also a student there, and probably didn't understand at all.

After dinner we finally got an Adam-reprieve. The intern went to work in Daddy's study, assuring us he would not intrude on our moonlight swim. I showed Jake to the guest quarters and went upstairs to slip into a bathing suit. I chose a latex two-piece from my Isaac Mizrahi swimwear collection.

By the time I was ready, Jake was out by the pool. My hottie was dipping his hand in to test the water temperature. It had to be several degrees lower than my body temperature. The vision of Jake in his bathing suit sent me into tummy quivers. He was beyond nice cuts. Well into what De dubs "six-pack abs"—taut muscles that resemble a six pack of soda cans.

"Nice, uh, bathing suit," I stammered. Like I'd even noticed his trunks.

"Likewise." Jake winked.

Then, without warning, he bounded over to the deep end, stretched his arms above his head, and executed a perfect running dive into the pool. His sculpted form sliced into the water. Breaking the surface a few yards later, he grinned and shook the water out of his eyes. "Coming in?"

I squiggled in, and together Jake and I swam side by side. We goofed around but couldn't chance being romantic. Hello, Adam was a few feet away—albeit behind the glass sliding doors.

But just being together in the pool was totally conducive to sharing. Mostly we talked about frothy stuff like our love for puppies and sorbet. But suddenly, Jake leaned up against the side of the pool and got serious. "I have a confession to make, Cher."

I tensed. For some bizarre reason, I flashed on that *People* magazine in Jake's car. Like maybe he had read it and really had known who I was but didn't want to say so. But not even.

"Remember I told you that my dad bolted? Well, my mom and I are still kind of working out the finances. That's why my credit card was rejected at Starbucks. And why getting in free to the concert . . . well, it was the only way we'd have gotten in. And that's why I didn't offer to pay for dinner tonight. I'm embarrassed about that."

Picturing some evil divorce, with Jake's mom in settlement limbo, I waded over and brushed Jake's water-logged locks out of his dewy eyes. "You have nothing to apologize for, Jake. I so understand. Daddy handles a million cases like that. Eventually, they all get settled."

In a steely voice, he said, "I know."

Then Jake reached out for me. He slipped his arm around my waist and started to pull me close. Smooch-op alert. Or would have been *if* the sliding door hadn't just opened, *if* the khaki-clad Adam hadn't come toddling out. Like *if* it wasn't for bad timing, that boy would have no timing at all.

"Sorry to interrupt again, Cher, but Mel's on the phone."

I bolted out of the pool and threw a towel around my shoulders. But not before Adam gave me an appreciative once-over. Hastily I said, "Thanks—I'll take it in Daddy's study."

Adam followed me in, whispering, "Don't worry, I didn't tell him you had company."

Again I went Ally McBeal. What I thought was, "Thanks for the solid: Daddy would have gone ballistic." But what I said was, "Whatever. You could have told him. Daddy trusts me."

Not that *I* told Daddy. Hello, it didn't come up. Instead, I gushed excitedly about my PSAT coup. Daddy was majorly pumped. "This calls for a celebration! I'm in Chicago now, but I'll be home by five o'clock on Friday night, so call out for dinner from your favorite place. And, Cher?"

I assumed Daddy was about to mention some congratulatory gift he might bring me in honor of my academic triumph, but not even. Instead, he said, "Could you put Adam back on the phone?"

Tragically, the next few days remained strained between me and my homies. My t.b.'s weren't outwardly hostile, just chilly. The way you feel in a mesh camisole during a Santa Ana wind event.

They all gave monosyllabic answers to my questions. Desperate for even a soupçon of our usual witty repartee, I actually fished for an Amber insult. But the walking fashion flaw couldn't even muster a misguided slur. This was bad.

If it wasn't for Jake, who counseled, "Give them time, they'll get over it," I might have suffered permanent emotional angst. Wonderful Jake: he was such my knight in Hilfiger armor, my Leonardo DiCaprio, saving me from titanic t.b. desertion. Jake drove me to school and when possible, took me home. On those rides we continued to share.

We so both believed in a relationship based on trust. And openness. We shared secrets. Jake told me about his strained finances; I told him that the streaks in my hair were totally Mascara Flair. It's like Buffy's friends knowing she's the slayer but never betraying her.

We talked in the car, we talked on the phone. But I wouldn't chance inviting him into my house again. Not with Adam the spy around. Just because he hadn't ratted me out that one time was no guarantee of continued discretion.

Jake was beyond understanding. On Friday afternoon when he picked me up from school, he ventured, "Listen, I've been to your house twice, and you haven't been to mine at all. How about coming over now?"

Now? I considered. It wasn't like I had other pressing plans. No mall troll with De was on the agenda. No nothing with De—or with any of my friends.

Before I committed, Jake shyly confessed, "My mother's been dying to meet you."

His *mom?* Meeting-his-mother panic engulfed me. Who knew, when dressing for school today, I might make an appearance in front of my potential future in-law? Jake continued, "My mom went all wicky-wacky when I told her who you were and who your dad was."

I echoed, "Wicky-wacky?"

Jake laughed. "Sorry, one of Mom's expressions. She's a little kooky."

Kooky *and* wicky-wacky? This could be a challenge

even the right clothes alone might not overcome. "Jake, you'd better debrief. Like, before we get there."

"Right. Okay, well, here's the thing. When I told Mom your name, she insisted she knows your dad."

I shrugged. "Well, you said that issue of *People* magazine in your car was hers. She probably remembers the Mel Horowitz article—"

"No," Jake interrupted. "I mean, as a friend. From the old days."

I was stunned. Like, if *I'd* been driving, screeching brakes would have been heard across the Southland. I gripped his arm. "And the reason you didn't mention this before would be . . . ?"

Jake checked the side-view mirror and pulled over to the curb.

"Mom can be intense," he explained. "She has a tendency to go overboard. I'm her only child, and she can't resist the urge to meddle in my life. So I wanted to keep her, you know, at bay. At least until I knew that, well, you and I were actually in a relationship. That it wasn't just one date and over."

Softly, I said, "I think we both know it's more than that."

Jake's sudden dental display dazzled me. "So, now the real test. You get to meet Mom. And if you still want to see me after that . . . Well, anyway, I take no responsibility for anything she says."

I grinned. "Color me warned."

Before pulling back onto the road, he whipped out his cellular and informed his mom of our impending visit. She didn't seem to mind unexpected company.

The Forrests had moved into a high-rise apartment building on Doheny Drive. While the address is *technically* zip-code appropriate, everyone who lives in Beverly Hills knows it's fully borderline.

As did Jake, who explained, "It's temporary. Just until we get settled. Most of our stuff is in storage."

"Say no more. Moving is such the trauma, I know."

He chuckled. "You do? But you've been in your house your entire life."

"How'd you know that?" I asked, surprised.

Jake shifted uncomfortably behind the wheel. "You told me, didn't you?"

Had I? It was possible. Whatever.

We took the elevator to the third floor, and Jake led me to apartment 3H.

Without missing a beat, he ushered me in and called out, "Mom! We're here."

Instantly, the aroma of a cooking smell enveloped me. What was it? Not something I'd ever sniffed in my own house, or in any of my friends'. Then it hit me. Hel*lo*, carbs! "Is someone baking bread?" I guessed.

But before Jake could answer, a trim, petite woman materialized.

Jake's mom. If I had to do a Pop-Up video balloon on her, it would say: "Nancy Reagan's collagen-challenged twin." Her sartorial style consisted of a classic Chanel suit in an obviously discontinued hue. And the fabric? Nubbiness is so not next to stylishness. At least her slingback stilettoes were of the now. Potentially.

Her dark hair was sprayed into a helmet-esque flip. I

hadn't realized how far behind the hair-times salons in San Diego must be. I made a mental note: should we bond in a follicular way, I would sponsor a visit with Jose Eber.

In spite of his mom's wardrobe and unfortunate hair, it was a cinch to see where Jake got his intense cobalt eyes. Hers were the matriarchal match of his.

Jake hastily did the intros.

"It's a pleasure to meet you, Mrs. Forrest," I said, extending my hand.

"Who's Mrs. Forrest?" she answered sweetly, gripping my hand firmly. "Call me Sandy." She nodded toward the kitchen. "I just popped some seven-grain bread into the micro and put up a pot of tea. I'll go check on it."

Jake shifted his weight and rubbed his hands together uncomfortably. "So, anyway, I'd show you around, but there's not much to see. All our stuff's in storage."

"Tscha, everything I need to see is standing right in front of me," I offered, taking his hand.

Jake blushed and led me to the dominating piece of furniture in the room: a pillow-obsessed, scratchy, brocade-covered couch. I totally sank into it and realized getting up gracefully would be a challenge.

Jake intuited my concern. "It's not my taste. The apartment came with it."

Jake did so not need to apologize. The apartment screamed "interim environment." It was viciously view-impaired. The living room window looked out over the parking garage.

I squeezed his hand supportively just as Mrs. Forrest—Sandy, that is—returned carrying a tray. On it sat a pot of steaming herbal tea and three cups. And a loaf of piping hot bread, accessorized by baby jars of jams and jellies. The kind they give out in first class. Or at IHOP.

Carefully placing the tray down on the IKEA-esque coffee table, she settled into a wing chair across from us. "So, Cher," Sandy started, pouring the tea into veiny thin china cups. "Jake's been sort of secretive about you. But you know how boys are. They never tell their parents anything. Unlike daughters." She winked at me. The crinkles around her eyes screamed for lasers.

I shot Jake a sidelong glance. "Just now, on the ride over here, Jake mentioned something about . . . you know my dad?"

Sandy nodded. "If it's the same Mel Horowitz, we go way back. Actually, I knew Diedre first. Your mother, that is."

She knew Mom? This was titanic! Atomic! Like Amber in an outfit that's actually in style. How had Jake withheld this vital info from me?

As we sipped tea and munched on the mouthwatering seven-grain bread, Sandy went into an amazing back story. "I met your mother in college. We were in the same sorority, Kappa Kappa Gamma." She stopped, pursing her lips at a sudden memory. "The boys, so immature, used to call it Visa Visa MasterCard."

I flashed on Murray and Sean—is that so not what

they would have said? Boyzone expressions are so predictable.

Sandy continued, chuckling. "I was actually there the day your mother met your father. It was at one of our sorority dinners. He was a waiter. Don't take this the wrong way, Cher, but even then it was clear Mel's talents lay elsewhere."

I felt all warm and fuzzy. Daddy had told me that he worked his way through law school as a waiter. And during a catered sorority dinner, he served Mom's table. But Daddy had never detailed the actual events. Now, to have Sandy go all eyewitness, was just like in the movie *Titanic,* when that old lady narrated the "I Was There" story.

Suddenly Sandy asked, "Would you like to see pictures, dear? I have several old sorority yearbooks in the bedroom."

Jake rolled his eyes. "Mom! I'm sure she doesn't! You're embarrassing Cher—not to mention probably boring her."

Not even! I was beyond buzzed at seeing snapshots of Sorority Mom. And like, hello, what an amazing stroke of luck—or fate—that Sandy's old sorority yearbooks weren't in storage with the rest of their belongings.

In fact, there were four leather-bound volumes, one for each year of college. In page after page of the Kappa Kappa Gamma yearbooks, there were snapshots of Mom, such the '70s Betty. Not unlike she appears in the portrait on our wall. Obviously, Jake had never seen his mom's yearbooks or he would have made the connection when he was at my house. And just like a boy, he wasn't interested in sitting through them now. Jake excused himself and went into his room.

I majorly kvelled as I viewed shots of Mom and her sorority sisters in all settings: outdoors, putting up banners announcing Rush Week; in the Kappa dorm, in hair rollers (!)—like, memo: give thanks for blow dryers—at a dance, wearing an amazing dress; even at a soup kitchen, serving meals to the homeless. And, hello, this was during the Me decade. Mom was such the before-her-time Betty, a pioneer in the pre-support ribbon era. But my favorite photos featured her hand-holding with a younger, unlined-face Daddy.

For the next several hours, Sandy did verbal captioning, fully regaling me with Mom tales. I was a captive audience. I couldn't get enough.

According to Sandy, it was she who sponsored Mom's membership in Kappa Kappa Gamma. "The other girls didn't see Diedre's potential. But I did."

And according to Sandy, she'd taken style-challenged Mom under her wing and taught her the fine art of fashion. "See that ensemble she's in?" Sandy pointed to a shot of Mom in a St. Laurent chemise and jacket. "I actually lent her that one."

She had? I'd always imagined Mom had the same instinctive good taste I did. But Sandy had been there. She had proof.

And bombshell alert. According to Sandy, if it wasn't for her coaxing, I might never have been born. "I was the one who promoted your mother's relationship with your father," she revealed.

"You mean it wasn't love at first sight . . . ?" I trailed off as another imagined fantasy was vanquished.

Sandy snorted. "Not close. I mean—let's see, how can I put this delicately? Your mother felt her dates had to meet certain standards."

"Standards?"

"She came from a cultured background," Sandy started, "as did all the Kappa girls."

I gulped. "Mom was a snob?"

She sniffed. "Snob? We never looked at it that way, Cher. But there was a sort of unwritten code. One didn't date out of one's station. Nor does one now."

"Out of one's station? You mean zip code?"

Sandy pursed her lips. "To be blunt, one didn't date the help. But I told her, 'DeeDee'—we all called her DeeDee. I said, 'DeeDee, you must look beyond his wait-staff status. His propensity for paunch. His use of words like *cockamamie*.' I told her to ignore the taunts, the behind-her-back snickers. I assured her she would not be kicked out of KKG. I pledged my personal guarantee." Sandy folded her hands in her lap and lifted her chin regally.

This was atomic. Mom was majorly lucky to have had a friend like Sandy. I mean, if she hadn't . . . if she'd never gone out with Daddy . . . I couldn't go there.

Jake interrupted the nostalgia session by coming back into the living room and tapping on his TAGHeuer. "It's after eight o'clock, ladies—do we know where our dinner is? Growing boys have to eat."

A flash of white-hot panic rocked me. "Eight

o'clock? Omigod, Daddy! He said he'd be home by five! I promised I'd be there, with dinner."

As I whipped out my cellular, I exclaimed to Sandy and Jake, "Come home with me! I can't wait for Daddy to meet you!"

But Sandy nixed my impulsive, "This isn't the right time. Your father just got back from a weeklong business trip. He'll be tired."

Grievously, she forgot to tack on, "And cranky."

Physically Daddy was home, but emotionally he was in Grump City. It wasn't a jet lag moment, either. Daddy was ballistic at my tardy. "I expected you to be here when I got home, Cher. Or at least to find a message or any indication of where you were. I called Dionne, but she didn't know. I called Murray and Sean and even Amber. No one knew where you were. You can't imagine what I've been thinking for the last few hours. I was just about to call Bill Krupke!"

The police? Daddy had gone all wicky-wacky with worry! I had to calm him down. "Chill, Daddy, I'm fine. I have a gold-plated excuse. Wait till you hear—"

Daddy brutally silenced me. "All I want to hear is the sound of your footsteps coming through the door. Our door. Now."

On the ride home, Jake fretted, "Your father really hates me now. First the car accident, now this."

"Tscha, Jake, totally temporary. When Daddy finds out why I lost track of time—and who you are, he'll be completely pumped. I can't wait to tell him!"

* * *

Tragically, Daddy could—hello, *insisted* upon—waiting. As in: he did not want an explanation of where I'd been. Nor did he listen with open ears when I tried to tell him about Sandy. And Mom. And like how serendipitous could it be that my soul mate turns out to be the son of Mom's former best t.b.?

But the worry lines in Daddy's face were deeper than I'd ever seen them. He growled, "Cher, I just got off a plane. I've been away for a week. I don't remember any old sorority sister of your mother's named Sandy. And right now I'm too preoccupied to think about it. I'm just glad you're safe. I've got to go through the files Adam pulled last week."

So that was it. Daddy chose to focus his energy on Adam and that old lawsuit, instead of me and my earth-shattering news. I felt shunted aside. Like that first McCaughey child when the septuplets came home.

Chapter 8

I went fully introverted all weekend. Only not by choice. I had no one to be extroverted with. My t.b.'s, still stung by the PSAT flap, hit the delete key on all my voice mails and E-mails.

Daddy was fully invested in Adam. I mean, in his old case files. All I heard were random swatches of conversation. About some Bobby Heller dude. And some law school test. And the statute of limitations. I wondered what the statute of limitations was on Daddy's affections. Had I exceeded them?

I knew better than to try to see Jake. Or even reopen conversations about him with Daddy. It's like that famous poem about discretion being the better part of valor. Or, possibly, the one about See no evil.

Whatever. I fully believe in my generation's motto, To thine own self, just be. Being Cher Horowitz means living in the solution.

So I spent my down time productively. After checking and updating all the personal information on my Web site, I identified all major dilemmas. Aside from world peace, feeding the hungry, and halting heinous experiments on helpless animals, there were two pressing problems. First, getting Daddy to acknowledge my existence and hear my volcanic news about Sandy—the woman who'd brought him together with Mom. Second, getting my t.b.'s back *and* getting them to meet Jake.

Tragically, Daddy was all Do not disturb. He barricaded himself in his study all weekend. Just him, Adam, and tons of old files. Even when I tiptoed in bearing little white boxes signifying Chinese food, all he managed was a perfunctory "Thanks, Pumpkin, we'll talk later."

So I fixated on my other quandary. I could not stand to live one more moment in two separate worlds. My friends and my boyfriend had to meet.

Wisely, I decided to focus on De. If she could just get over the hump of PSAT-trauma, we would be on the road to recovery. And where De led? Murray and Sean were sure to follow. As for Amber, where else did she have to go?

But how to do it? After many intense hours of obsessing, I realized that an olive branch was the answer. So I went out and bought De a gift: *The Girlfriends Keepsake Book: The Story of Our Friendship*.

It's the one where you fill in the blanks about the cool things you and your best t.b. did together. I spent all day Sunday writing in our most amusing childhood anecdotes. For the I Knew We Would Be Friends page, I wrote about the day we first met. It was kindergarten, and we realized we were destined to be the most popular girls throughout all of public school. We bonded.

I wrote about other rites of passage. About the time we got our first credit cards, our nascent lipstick experiences, our trip to Paris, our unexpected camping encounter, my bat mitzvah, De's confirmation. To illustrate, I pasted in memory snapshots. Just those shots of me and De in our most heinous haircuts had to jolt De out of her resentment. And remind her that our decade-long girlfriend bond should not be cast asunder by a PSAT score.

When I was done, I called Jake and convinced him to have lunch with us in the Quad on Monday. At first my hottie was reluctant, concerned that my friends wouldn't like him. But I assured him, hello, not even. How could anyone not immediately fall head over feet for Jake Forrest, studmuffin supreme, dude of my dreams?

Hope sprang internal when I arrived at school on Monday morning. Until, that is, externally I spied a pre-homeroom De in the Quad. In a flash, my optimism ebbed.

For my main big was tragically wearing her heartbreak on her . . . I couldn't be sure, but it looked like T-Shirt in a Can. Worse, she had on boot-cut pants with platforms! The whole look cried, "I got this out of the Delia catalogue and I'm so bummed, I don't care who knows!"

De having a fashion implosion? Egregious emotional crisis alert! I had no time to waste. Boldly, I approached her. Blindly, I didn't mention her hideous ensemble. Hopefully, I gave her the *Girlfriends Keepsake Book*. Tentatively, she took it.

And finally, I felt her begin to resuscitate.

Perched on a bench in the Quad, De flipped through the pages. Slowly, her face began to register cheerful emotions. The corners of her lips gradually turned up. The pall over her eyes lifted. When she giggled? I knew she'd taken the first steps back toward our friendship. When, spying the page on my bat mitzvah—hello, we were twelve!—she burst out in full hysterics, I knew we were patched. I let out a sigh of relief that nearly drowned out the homeroom bell.

During our morning classes, De and I made up for our lost week. We communed. I updated her on my relationship with Jake. It was way laborious because I had to do it via creative writing in first-period Express Yourself class. Then I had to explain it all *"En français, sil vous plaît,"* as our teacher commanded in second period.

De was all eyes and ears. She gasped audibly—in a major *"Mon dieu!"* manner—when I described the colossal kismet of Jake's mom having been my mom's best friend.

By third period De was finally able to divulge. That's

when she admitted the real angst behind her week-long shut down. It wasn't just about *me* trouncing her. So had half the school!

De's exquisite hazel eyes misted when she bitterly croaked, "Cher, I totally tanked on the math part. It was full-score meltdown."

I didn't know what to say. So, instead of saying nothing, I went with stupid. I announced, "Oh, De, what is a PSAT anyway? How can it even compare to other initials in our lives? Like DKNY? Or cK? BCBG? FUBU . . ." Alas, even to my own ears, the anagram recitation rang hollow.

De shot me a look. "You're overcompensating, Cher. We all know exactly what those initials mean. If I don't vastly improve on the SATs, I can kiss my dreams of medical school good-bye . . ."

". . . and start practicing the phrase 'I'll take that bedpan for you, Doctor.'" Sean, who should have been safely seated behind me, had gotten up and stuck his head between ours. But a swift elbow to comic boy's abdomen forced him to back off.

I shook my head vehemently. "No way, De! I see a world where we are not judged by PSAT scores alone. I see a world where PSAT scores will fail to strike fear in the hearts of juniors across America. Where our entire futures will no longer be number-dependent . . ."

Jarringly, Amber—and I include her blue-hued wig in that description—leaned toward us and intruded. "Easy for you to say, Miss I Ruled the PSATs."

I turned back to De. The look on her face was all I needed to see. The enormity of my main's crash-and-burn performance finally sank in. All week De had been plagued with self-doubt. Like, what if she wasn't as brain-worthy as she'd always thought? What if she didn't have the chops to go into medicine? It's been her only dream since Amber's original nose.

I was gripped with regret. De had been so needing me. Only not me, because I was the one who took those top honors away from her. It's like when your best friend is dumped by her boyfriend and you want to be there for her, only you can't be because you've hooked up with him. Or something.

Intuiting De's potential slide into self-doubt, Murray bounded out of his seat and put a consoling arm around his boo. "It's okay, baby. It's gonna be all right. Come on, De, chant with me now, just like we practiced: 'I get knocked down . . . but I get up again . . .'"

Murray motioned for everyone to join in, and the whole class did, even Mrs. DeMicco. Only De's whisper of that Chumbawamba chant was tragically pathetic.

Murray coaxed, "And when you're finished with all that test stuff, every Ivy League college and medical school in the country will be after you. It'll be like the NBA draft."

I beamed. Murray dropped his immature drool-boy persona to come through in an emotional crunch. It gives ultimate credence to his soul mate worthiness.

I gave him a thumbs-up. "That is such the spirit, Murray. How can I help?"

"Just keep hope alive, Cher, and believe in second chances. Believe—"

Snarkily, Amber interjected, "In the power of our parents' considerable influence."

I groaned. "Amber, give it up. Our parents' financial resources are but a minor advantage. We can make it on our own, in spite of setbacks."

Murray silenced me. "No, that's not what she means. A group of our parents got together and fought for a retest. In two weeks we get to take the PSATs again. The scores we got the first time will be scrapped."

I was stunned. I stammered, "Y-You're getting a do-over?"

Sean confirmed. "Only those students who want to. Which is all of us—except you."

I swallowed. In all my years in academia, the only time I'd ever heard of retesting was due to some gross misconduct, like if someone had cheated or gotten hold of the answers before the test. Nervously, I inquired, "On what exact grounds are you getting the do-over?"

Amber, filing her nails, explained. "First of all, Cher, please stop calling it a do-over. This is not potsy or hopscotch. It's merely an adjustment."

"An adjustment? Like moving a shoulder pad? I repeat, why *are* you getting to retake it?"

Amber rolled her eyes. "Excuse me, the conditions we took the test under were unfair. Grossly counter-productive."

They were? Only if you were hypnotized that day by Amber's outfit.

De sniffed, rationalizing, "There *were* external

noises. Coming from the football field adjacent to the testing room. It was distracting. To some of us."

"De? Do you really believe that?"

De averted direct eye contact with me. "Of course I do, Cher. And this time, with fewer distractions and more preparation, I'm bound to end up with a score that's more reflective of my true aptitude. Probably."

Murray supported her. "Not probably. Definitely. But just to be sure, De signed up for a tutoring course."

Sean added, "We all signed up. Murray, me, even Amber."

In spite of my reservations about the whole do-over thing, I wanted to be supportive. Briefly, I considered joining the tutoring encounter. But then I realized that, hello, what if I retook the test and did even better? Would that not be the biggest nah-nah-nah-nah-nah?

So I did the next best thing. I suggested, "De, how about a shopping spree this afternoon? To celebrate second chances."

But De shook her head and closed her math book. "No can do, Cher. I have to study. The tutor gave us stuff to prepare for the first session."

I hid my disappointment. "Say no more. I understand. Just remember, De, I'm always here for you at the other end of the pager. And, De? I'm sorry for outscoring you. Jake says——"

Just then the bell rang, and De darted to her next class. If I didn't know better, I'd think De didn't really want to hear what Jake said.

* * *

Later, settling into our reserved lunch table in the Quad, I felt more juiced than I had in days. My friends and I were patched, Jake was in my life, and soon my two worlds would be one. De, Murray, Sean, and Amber didn't know it yet, but they were about to meet my soul mate. I didn't even realize I was warbling that Spice Girls classic, *"If you wanna be my lover, you gotta get with my friends,"* until Murray, who slid onto the bench next to De, tilted his head and squinted at me. "The Spice Girls? What's that about, Cher?"

De, picking up my tuneful theme, pointed a plastic fork at me and sang out, *" "Tell us what you want, what you really, really want!" "*

Sean eyed my lunch tray suspiciously. "Mo' better, tell us what's up with the twin thing. Look what she's got. Two personal pizzas, two lattes, and two cookies. Should we be building an ark? Is there a storm approaching?"

Only El Niño in heels—Hurricane Amber—I thought, as our wildly dressed t.b.-by-default encroached on our VIP table. Her Highness was trailed by a subservient and sweaty freshman whom she'd bullied into carrying her tray. Dismissing the intimidated frosh, she injected a patented derogatory remark. "Love means never having to say you're hungry. Cher is in love, you know, with walking boy."

Nothing could bum me out, especially not Amber. But I did counter, "Hello, Ambu-tard, Jake owns a rampantly respectable sport ute. An Acura SLX if you have to know. The day you stalked us, it so happens we *opted* to walk. So we could stop and smell the palm trees. So we could hold hands, gaze into each other's eyes as the gentle breeze . . ."

Amber stuck out her tongue and mimed hurling. "Stop her before I gag."

I chortled. "Mock me all you want, but the truth is out there. In fact . . ."

I gazed toward the parking lot. A wide grin spread across my face. "The truth, draped in an excellent Hilfiger, is upon us."

I pointed at the primo studmuffin walking our way. My Jake.

My t.b.'s flipped around. Their eyes went wide. Wider when Jake came over to me, put his arm around my shoulders, and planted a peck on the top of my head. "Hi, baby," he said.

"Hi yourself," I said adoringly, patting the space on the bench next to me. "I picked up a pizza for you. Veggie, the way we both like it."

Then I turned to my friends. "This is—"

Amber didn't let me finish. She bolted vertical. "Jake!" she exclaimed, extending her sharp mani-claws in his direction. "How enchanting to see you again. Did you walk all the way here?"

Jake reached out and took her hand. "Amber, right?"

Despite Amber, the next forty-eight minutes was the most stellar lunch period I'd had all semester. Over all the necessary food groups—croissandwiches, piz-zas, salads, burgers, iced tea, and light-froth lattes, which Jake jokingly called coffee—my t.b.'s and my Jake fully blended.

We covered all the major getting-to-know-you topics. Where Jake was from, and did he know Sean's fourth cousin who also lived in San Diego? Or De's aunt whose boyfriend ran a surf shop on the bay? Jake didn't, but he did bond with the boys—he was a full Lakers fanatic like Murray and Sean. And big surprise—not—he charmed Amber and De. It seemed as if Jake had been part of our crowd forever. I felt whole.

The rest of the week was full swoon ahead. Although Daddy was still brutally preoc and my t.b.'s furiously invested in that crash PSAT tutoring course, Jake was there, nourishing me with soul mate sustenance.

On Tuesday we held hands, bared toes, and strolled the beach at sunset. Being with Jake, I barely obsessed about the frizz factor.

Wednesday after school we went for that picnic at Griffith Park that Jake had suggested when we first met. Catering from Spago Picnic Basket totally reduced the hokeyness element.

On Thursday we rented videos and watched them at Jake's house. My hottie is so enlightened, he agreed to my choices of *My Best Friend's Wedding* and *Jerry Maguire*. We even sang along—really badly—to those movie songs "I Say a Little Prayer" and "Secret Garden." We even acted out the talking part of the last one.

But mostly we cuddled on the couch.

When Sandy came home, I cajoled her into sharing more Mom stories. It wasn't hard to get her started.

She seemed to have an unending supply. Sandy painted a picture of a Mom I never really imagined. A less than secure Mom, but a Betty with a good heart, who got stronger with help from her t.b.'s. Especially one true blue.

That day, when Jake drove me home, I revisited the subject of his dad. Had he been the love of Sandy's life as Daddy had been the love of Mom's?

Jake's tense body language told me he didn't really want to go there. He only admitted that his parents, like mine, had met in college. But he didn't elaborate. He never said if his dad was in a fraternity or maybe was a waiter like Daddy. Whatever. I could wait until Jake was ready to share more.

During the rest of the drive, I ruminated about Daddy. "I so want you to meet him, Jake. We have to tell him who you really are."

The way he said, "All in good time, Cher," sounded odd. If I didn't know better, I'd even call it ominous. All the stress about Daddy must have made me misinterpret.

I sighed. "It's just that I've never seen Daddy so bombastic over a random case. If there was only some way we could help. It would solve everything. Daddy would find out how righteous you are, and his case woes would be over."

Jake went contemplative. "You know, Cher, from everything you've told me, it sounds like your dad has all the help he needs in Adam."

I fully bristled. "As if! If Adam's so bright, why are

they no closer to a wrap? It's been like, weeks. I can't understand why Daddy's being so lock-out about our offer to help."

We came to a red light. Slowly, Jake depressed the brake and ventured, "Is it possible Mel's being stubborn about Adam for another reason?"

"What other reason?"

Jake cleared his throat and looked straight ahead. "I'm no psych major or anything. But it sounds as if your dad really likes this Adam kid. Cher . . ." He paused. "You have no brothers, right?"

"What are you getting at?"

He inhaled. "Probably nothing. Probably I'm reaching. But sometimes my mom gets all wistful that she never had a daughter. Maybe your dad sees the son he never had in Adam. A struggling law student, just like he used to be."

The light changed and Jake hit the gas. We drove the rest of the way in silence. Could Jake be right? Did Daddy see Adam that way? I had to think of a way to make Daddy see me that way. I had to think of a way to make him proud of me.

On Saturday the way came to me. Jake and I had plans to go shopping. Without De, I'd been suffering from mall deprivation, and Jake selflessly agreed to keep me company.

I'd overheard Daddy tell Adam to meet him at Horowitz & Associates' downtown office. So I knew the coast would be clear for a few hours at least. When Jake came to pick me up, I invited him in.

"Are you sure?" he asked nervously, lingering in the doorway.

"As sure as I am of you and me, Jake."

Following me inside, he casually mentioned, "You know, Cher, last time I was here, I noticed a painting in your dad's study. I think it's a Picasso, but I didn't get a good look at it. Any chance I could . . ."

Before Jake could finish his sentence, I led him through the foyer, and into Daddy's home office. I stopped short. The place was clutter chic. All the old files Daddy had gotten out of storage totally dotted the floor and even the couch. We had to climb over them to get to the Picasso.

Jake admired it but then found something else to admire more: me. He took my hands and waxed ecstatic. "What is it that I love about you? You can turn the world on with your smile. You can take a nothing day and suddenly make it all seem worthwhile . . ."

While that sounded somewhat familiar—Nick at Night-esque—there was no mistaking the sincerity in Jake's eyes. He meant every word. And then I remembered what Madame Tiara had told me about my soul mate. Had she not said he'd appreciate my generous spirit?

I leaned my head against his chest, and he put his arm around me and nuzzled my neck.

Looking over Jake's shoulder is when it occurred to me. If the mountain won't come to Mohammed Ali . . .

Chapter 9

Am I not such the mountain mover? Without heavy machinery, I could bring a massive mountain of evidence to Daddy. Evidence that proved Jake and I could help him. Better than Adam. And then I could finally tell Daddy who Jake really was. And, bonus, reintroduce him to Sandy.

Okay, so I didn't know anything about the heinous Heller case, except that it was old—the files had been in deep storage—but I trusted Jake. Like my horoscope predicted, my soul mate had a sharp, intuitive mind. I knew he could help.

When I told Jake my brilliant idea, *he* went Ally McBeal. He stammered, "Are you s-sure we're doing the right thing?" But there was no hiding the tingling he felt. He knew we were about to do the right thing. The only thing.

And so, Jake and I started going through all the old

storage boxes in Daddy's office. We pulled out all the files marked Heller. We made copies of everything, then put the originals back in the boxes. It was way labor-intense, since there were tons of files.

When we were done, I reminded him about our shopping date, but Jake begged off. "This is a lot of stuff to go through. I'd better get started."

I grinned at his eagerness. "Don't you mean, *we?* We're a team, Jake. Let's take all this stuff out on the deck. I'll get highlighters."

I started to open a drawer to get some in pink and yellow, but Jake grasped my elbow. "I don't think so, Cher. We can't work here. What if your dad comes home? He hasn't listened to a word you've said so far—he'd go ballistic if he saw us. Let me take these files home. I'll start with the boring parts, organizing everything. Then we'll work together on the important items."

I wanted to protest that I didn't mind helping out on the boring parts. But Jake suddenly pulled me to him and gave me a kiss that left no room for protest. My knees nearly buckled.

I helped him carry the files out to his car. In his eagerness to get going, Jake practically made skid marks on the driveway. His parting words were reassuring. "Don't worry, Cher. I'll call you later, and we'll work on this together."

But he didn't call. Not the rest of that day or the next or the one after. When I called him, Jake hastily explained that he'd gotten so bogged down in the files, he didn't have time to talk. He wasn't ready for my highlighting skills.

"Daddy's case is that complicated?"

He paused. "More than I could have imagined. I need time to do this right. I *have* to make a good impression on your dad. It's really important to me now, Cher, because—"

"Because what, Jake?"

He swallowed. "Because I think I'm in love with you, Cher. Because I think I want to spend the rest of my life with you. And right now your dad hates me. There's only one way to turn that around. If I make a killer impression on him by coming in with stuff to help him break this case, imagine how he'd feel about me then? He'd do a total one-eighty. He'd give our relationship his blessing. It's what I want more than anything."

"It's what I want, too, Jake," I whispered.

"So just give me a little more time to work on this by myself," he implored. "I want to impress you, too, Cher."

"You already have, Jake."

I promised myself I wouldn't call for at least a few more days. But after two, I couldn't help myself. This time Sandy answered. She sounded surprised that Jake and I hadn't spoken in a while. Knowing that boys tell their moms nothing, I filled her in. Sandy listened intently and agreed that giving Jake more research time was the best idea.

Before I hung up, I blurted, "Sandy—you *have* to

come over! Maybe Daddy's been too preoccupied to listen to me, but if he saw *you,* imagine how pumped he'd be!"

Sandy demurred. "Your heart is in the right place, Cher, but speaking from a parent's point of view, I know what it's like to be preoccupied with a work matter. And sometimes surprises aren't as welcome as you'd think. Why don't we just wait a little longer."

"I know!" I exclaimed. "The minute Jake even comes up with one micro-mini idea for Daddy's case, that's when you'll both come over. Daddy has to welcome that surprise."

While I waited for Jake to finish organizing, I decided to redouble my efforts to get through to my stress-addled pop. I scheduled a session with Fabianne, only the most booked-up masseuse in Beverly Hills who makes house calls. If Daddy tragically refused to partake? I could use some destressing, too.

But miraculously Daddy actually agreed. "A half-hour session, Cher. That's all the time I can spare," he said, then added softly, "Look, honey, I'm sorry I've been so busy. I know you've been trying to talk to me. I just haven't had time to really listen."

On Saturday we did an actual father-daughter quality time encounter. That's when Fabianne set up her massage-to-go center in the family room. I sat on the couch and talked to Daddy as Fabianne, aided by the aromatherapy candles I'd lit, worked on his back. Finally, he really listened.

I told him more about Jake, how we'd just clicked from the moment we met. Daddy's first response was to make a grumbling noise about my car.

"It'll be ready this week, Daddy, and you'll totally see how Jake took care of the insurance issue." I didn't add the part about Hal deducting stuff. That would be a surprise.

Daddy didn't seem to have the energy to protest. So I took a deep breath and finally broke my earth-shattering news to him. The news I'd been trying to tell him for weeks: I told him about Sandy.

Slowly, Daddy lifted his head off the massage table. "Pumpkin, I told you before. I never knew a Sandy Forrest."

Well, duh, Forrest was her married name. Of course Daddy wouldn't know it. So I described Sandy, especially as she'd looked in the old pictures. I reminded him about the Kappa Kappa Gamma connection.

"Well, naturally I remember the sorority," Daddy said, smiling as Fabianne's magic thumbs dug into his shoulder blades. "After all, it was at her sorority dinner that your mom and I met."

"That's just it, Daddy. Sandy encouraged Mom to go out with you."

Daddy chuckled. "I don't seem to remember her needing any encouragement."

"But, Daddy—"

He heaved a major sigh. "Your mother was very popular and had a lot of sorority sisters. And understand, Cher, if I don't want to take a trip down memory lane just now. The cockamamie Heller mess takes me right back to those days—and in case you haven't noticed, it's been pretty upsetting."

"But Sandy was Mom's closest friend. Wait till you see the pictures! And segue, maybe Sandy and Jake can even help with the case." I said it lightly, so Daddy wouldn't guess that Jake already had the files in hand.

Daddy tensed. "Cher, no. I told you when all this began, I don't want you meddling. It's too complicated."

I back-pedaled. "Okay, forget the case. But I want to invite them over."

Daddy groaned as Fabianne applied pressure to his lower back. "Okay, Cher, invite them over."

I brightened. "I will! And, Daddy, you will so love Jake. He's my other half. The half that wants to follow in your legal footsteps and be a lawyer someday. He's bright. He's thoughtful and caring. He loves the Beach Boys. And he's fully committed to human rights. He wants to save Tibet! Two weeks ago, on Monday night, we went to this concert—"

Like, major oops.

Oops squared.

In my delirium about finally being able to tell Daddy about Jake, I accidentally slipped and mentioned Tibetan Freedom. As in, we'd gone to the concert. On a school night. On a school night when Daddy was out of town.

All the tension-relieving benefits of the massage were abruptly rendered null and void at that second. Daddy bolted up. The vein in his forehead throbbed. He went into a Dennis Miller-worthy rant. "You did what? You went where? You disobeyed—and then lied about it when I called you? What's gotten into you, Cher?"

I struggled to keep my voice whine-free. "But, Daddy, weren't you even listening? It was for a good cause. And Jake's my soul mate."

"Your soul mate? He's some stranger who smashed into your car! And then influenced you to break my rules! You're right, Cher, I haven't been listening. I haven't been paying nearly as much attention to you as I should be. You need much more supervision."

"Not even, Daddy."

Tragically, he was off and raving. "Don't 'not even' me, Cher. This is completely unlike you. Or maybe I've been too lenient. I can't trust you anymore."

Suddenly, the stress of the past few weeks hit me, tsunami-like. I blurted, "Or maybe I'm just not the child you wanted. I'm not a boy. I'm not Adam."

I barely heard Daddy going, "Wha-a-a-t?"

My lip fully trembling, I grabbed my Prada gold-chain backpack and bolted out the door.

Okay, so my running-away skills *are* profoundly rusty. My only previous experience goes back an entire decade. When I was seven, Daddy wouldn't let me stay up past my bedtime to watch *The Little Mermaid* again. So I packed my pajamas, my silk sheets, and my Barbie dolls, and slipped out the back door. I "ran" two blocks away to De's. Tragically, her dad brought me right back home.

I wouldn't make the same mistake twice. De's house would be the first place Daddy would look. And I needed to put some space between me and my postal *père*.

What I needed more was a car, only mine was still detained at that body shop. I briefly considered taking Daddy's. But that might undermine the seriousness of my angst. Or make it worse.

I had no choice. I bolted as fast as my strappy four-inch platforms could take me. All I had were my wits, my wallet, and my makeup.

And my cellular. On which I called Jake. "Be there!" I implored as the phone rang once, twice, three times. Not even the voice mail picked up.

I tried Murray, but he was at a tutoring session. Which meant that De, Sean, and even Amber, were occupied too. I thought about crashing their session, but I didn't know where it was held.

I rounded the corner onto Sunset Boulevard and looked up. I was a block away from the pink and palm-tree-addled Beverly Hills Hotel, site of many a festive soiree that Daddy and I have attended over the years. Out by the main entrance is where taxis live. I bolted up the driveway and gave the driver an address I knew well in Santa Monica.

I ran away to Grandma Ray's.

I knew, hello, that she would totally call Daddy. But so would any of my friends' parents. Grandma, at least, would not boot me. She'd provide a safe haven. Unconditional-cum-overbearing love. Support. And food. Enough to feed a small third-world country.

True to form, she was grasping a tin of noodle pudding when she answered the door. Her electric blue eye shadow nearly blinded me. "Cher!" she exclaimed, and quickly lapsed into Grandma-speak. "*Tatela,* what a surprise. You look hungry. I was just preparing dinner. Come, *es mein kind.*"

I felt all my tension spontaneously release. It was good to be in a place where nothing ever changes. Grandma Ray—it's Rachel, but I call her Ray—believed in being prepared, as if an army of hungry relatives might storm in unannounced. She was supremely turned out, as usual. As I followed her inside, I remarked favorably on her vintage Geoffrey Beene pants suit from his resortwear collection. "You'd never know it's elastic waist."

I couldn't refrain from a mini-critique of her coif, though. Sprayed into oblivion, it looked like it could be home to a large swarm of bees. Gently, I offered to make an appointment with Jose Eber.

But Grandma could see right through me. Especially after she slipped her harlequin reading glasses onto her nose. "Cher, you didn't come here to talk about my hair. I know you love my cooking, but that's not why you're here, either. And since Melvin isn't with you, I can only surmise you had maybe a slight miscommunication with your father, am I right?"

I planted myself at Grandma's gray-speckled Formica kitchen table. Do they even make those anymore? It might be an antique, I mused. Before I could ask, she set a steaming bowl of yellow liquid before me. Islands of fat floated on top. As I expertly skimmed them off, I suddenly understood why those schmaltzy chicken soup books are so popular. It was over a bowl of that, enhanced with Grandma's rocket-size matzo balls, that I spilled everything to her. I fully cleansed my soul.

I complained about how Daddy had been bogged down with some heinous blast-from-the-past case and only listened to Adam. Even after I provided a destressing massage session, he still ignored me.

Grandma stood at the stove and stirred some gravy for the pot roast in the oven. Knowingly, she said, "Don't be so hard on your father, Cher. Maybe things aren't so good for him right now. I remember some of those old cases, before Mel got famous. They were terrible."

Grandma suddenly got a faraway look in her eyes. "There was one case that was the worst. I don't remember the name or the details, just the letters your mother wrote about it."

"She wrote you letters? Why?"

"If I remember it right, it was when I was married to Harold—you remember him, *tatela*, your fourth step-grandpa? The one who fancied himself an artist? Anyway, Harold and I lived in Italy for a few months then. Your mother wrote me letters about some backstabbing friend who got into some trouble. Oy, it was horrible for her and for your father."

A flash of tenderness enveloped me. Mom and Grandma had been way close.

"Anyway, Cher, pooh-pooh, it's not for you to be concerned. Your father is a smart man. He'll figure it out. So, whatever it is he won't listen to you about? Have a slice of noodle pudding and tell me. I'm all ears."

I told Grandma all about Jake.

She smiled knowingly. "This Jake. He sounds like, what do you kids say, a cutie patootie?"

I giggled. "That's Rosie O'Donnell, Grandma. We say a hottie."

She nodded. "That's what I said, a hootie patootie. Go on."

I told Grandma about Sandy and all the kismet coincidences. I repeated all the tales Sandy had told me. I described the pictures. Although Grandma never stopped stirring the gravy, I knew she was listening to everything I said. Mainly because, when I was finished, she contradicted it. All of it.

About Mom's sorority: "Yes, your mother was in that Kappa Kappa Gamma sorority, but the boys didn't poke fun like that. They couldn't have called it Visa Visa MasterCard. There was no Visa in those days. Only American Express. And BankAmericard. And Master Charge. Trust me, this I would know."

About Mom's t.b.'s: "She never had a friend named Sandy."

About Mom's social life: "The boys were banging down the door for your mother. She was very popular, like you, Cher. But when she started up with Mel, it was hard. All her so-called friends, her snobby sorority sisters, turned their backs when she started dating him. A lowly waiter. From no money . . ."

I piped up, "Except for Sandy, right, Grandma? She didn't turn her back."

"Sandy? Cherela, I told you, I don't remember any Sandy. Before she met Mel, her best friend was a girl named Donna. They were together everywhere. And that hanger-on was always there—you know, like that Amber girl is always around you and Dionne. This girl, Alexondra she called herself. Not Alexandra, the way her parents had it on her birth certificate. She had to be fancy. But your mother knew Alexondra was just a social climber. And two-faced at that. She kept telling your mother, 'He's not good enough for you. He's a waiter, for heaven's sake.' And then what does she do? Goes and marries another waiter! A law student who was Melvin's friend. And they both made big trouble for your parents later on."

Point by point, Grandma refuted nearly everything Sandy had told me. I felt icky all over. Maybe Grandma Ray was losing it. Maybe everything changes, after all.

Whatever. I was too tired to protest when Grandma insisted on calling Daddy to tell him where I was. Although she did honor my request not to talk to him. She also insisted I stay the night. I hadn't brought any clothes, so I borrowed Grandma's nightgown. It was so not from Victoria's Secret. Flannel, with a ruffled collar, it totally put me in touch with my inner *Little House on the Prairie*. Maybe that's why it gave me weird dreams.

I dreamt I was on a softball field. Playing Little League ball. I was pitching. I could hear Daddy cheering from the stands, "Come on! You can do it! That's my kid!"

Only when I looked up, his eyes weren't on me. He was cheering for someone else. Adam was at bat.

Chapter 10

The next morning I was brutally awakened by the sun streaming through Grandma's mini-blind-challenged window. I squinted and pulled the covers over my head, but I couldn't fall back to sleep. I knew I had a choice to make. Go back home or hang with Grandma for a while.

I hit the mental playback button and heard Daddy's postal all over again. I chose Grandma, knowing full well that the decision could potentially be artery-clogging. Naturally Grandma saw it as an opportunity to "put a little meat on your bones." She was thrilled. She even agreed to accompany me home—when Daddy wasn't there, since I didn't want to face him—so I could get some essentials. School books, ensembles, accessories, cosmetics. The charger for my cellular.

I called Jake to tell him where I was if he needed me,

but he still didn't. "I'm getting closer, Cher. I can feel it. Hang on, it won't be long now."

My friends were sympathetic to my plight. De agreed to drive out of her way to pick me up for school. But that's pretty much all she could do. The PSAT crash course she and my homies were taking was majorly intense. It was like, all they thought or talked about.

During and between classes, they quizzed one another. De and Sean were all about square roots and those same two trains leaving different stations at the same time and when would they pass? Or something.

Murray and Amber worked nonstop on vocabulary. I tried to be part of it. But whenever I tried to interject a real-life anecdote, they were all, "Cher, enough about crush boy. We've got to work."

After two days at Grandma's, I heard the mother ship calling me home. The compartment where my clothes live, that is. Hello, I had no clue how sartorially stifled I'd be without continuous access to my closet. Woefully, Grandma wasn't available to drive me. She had a canasta game. Instead, she insisted I borrow the Grandma-mobile, a huge, canary yellow econo-box, circa Florida. Not the South Beach part. The geezer part.

And like that famous axiom about cars taking on the characteristics of their owners, the Grandma-mobile had an ancient mind of its own. As in, a speed limit it wouldn't go over. No matter how hard I pressed the accelerator, it totally mocked me. Which is why it took me close to an hour to make what should have been a twenty-minute drive.

On the way, I planned what I would say to Daddy. He was probably profoundly remorseful about going postal on me. He probably wanted to reopen the whole subject of trust. And what did I mean about not being the child he really wanted? But until I could get him to actually meet Jake, I wouldn't go there. I'd stay the course. Whatever that meant.

A potential interface with Daddy turned out to be fully moot anyway, since he didn't appear to be home. His car was gone.

But his usual parking space was very much occupado. So was mine and the guest spot next to it. The vehicles in our driveway were way recognizable: a Beemer, a 'Vette, a Jag, and a putt-putt car. Translation: Murray, De, Sean, Amber, and Adam were all at my house. But why?

Maybe because I was coming from Grandma's, but I suddenly went into this time-warp regression memory. I flashed on that classic little Golden book the Three Berenstain Bears fairy tale. Were they all in my house eating my porridge? And segue, what is porridge?

The mystery intensified when I went inside. I stood poised in our marble-tiled bodacious front hallway, listening. Their voices were coming not from the kitchen, but from the family room, and they sounded just like they did in school.

Murray was quizzing De on vocabulary. "Define *individuality*."

De demanded, "Could you possibly give me a less challenging one? Individuality is everything. It's in the juxtaposition of a chunky belt and a delicate jeweled choker. It's a brilliant blue lining, or a wispy braid."

Murray wasn't in my line of vision, but I could totally picture him rolling his eyes as he shot back, "Or a wispy *brain,* Dionne. I think I can say with authority that will *not* be one of the multiple choices on the test."

I walked over and peeked inside the family room just in time to see De strike a pose. She was kneeling on the floor, next to the marble, chrome, and glass coffee table. Hand on her hip, she threw Murray a patented expression of annoyance. I tingled with anticipation. A De–Murray contretemps was about to begin.

Listening to them—eavesdropping on them—I got all nostalgic. It wasn't so long ago that I was *in* the loop here. Now, here I was, an interloper in my own house. I was about to make my presence known when I heard footsteps behind me. Even if I hadn't noticed his demi-vehicle in the driveway, I would have ID'ed him.

And as he brushed by me, Adam was all, "Want to sit in on this session, Cher? I know you aced both parts of the PSAT, but you never know—even you might find my strategy sessions useful."

I spun around. *"Your* strategy sessions? What's this about? And why is everyone here?"

De, Murray, Sean, and Amber looked up at me, realizing for the first time that I was even there. They didn't seem shocked. De explained. "Adam's our PSAT

127

tutor. We assumed you knew that." If I hadn't been so preoccupied lately, I totally would have made the connection sooner.

I didn't answer. There was a lot about the multitalented Adam I didn't know. Including, why is he even in my life? Let alone tutoring my friends at my house. He explained, "Since I've been so busy working for your dad, he suggested holding today's session here to cut down on traveling time."

I looked from De to Murray to Sean to Amber. The first two were on the plush gray carpet nestled around the coffee table, books open and papers scattered around. Sean was stretched out on the floor next to them, his book akimbo, his pen poised in the air. Amber had commandeered the couch. She'd surrounded herself with audiotapes and piles of vocabulary cards.

"So, Cher," Adam said again, striding over to my homies. "You want to sit in? No charge."

I felt profoundly out of place, like Michael J. Fox in the Big & Tall store. "No thanks, I'll just . . ." I never finished the sentence. I turned on my heel and bolted upstairs to gather the sartorial supplies I'd come for. I didn't bother saying good-bye when I left a few minutes later for the hideously long, slow drive back to Grandma's. There I did something I never do. I sunned myself outside by her condo pool. Without sunscreen.

"Hold up, Cher!" Murray and Sean, the citrus twins—the former was in an orange crushed velvet Vneck, the latter in a blinding lime jacket—came flying at me the next day in school as I was tossing some books into my locker. De and Amber were right behind them.

Murray, nearly out of breath, accused me, "You been ducking us all morning."

Technically, that was true. I'd made it all the way to third period without one significant t.b. interface. But I didn't think they'd noticed.

"Avoidance is so not the answer," Amber interjected. "Especially when you do it. It's transparent."

I lifted my chin. "Transparent? You mean like that faux sarong wrapped around your waist? Tip: on Fiona, it's edgy; on you, merely edge of schlock."

De narrowed her eyes and grasped my chin. Inspecting my face, she guessed. "No sunscreen chez Grandma? Cher, you need moisturizer." De dug inside her Coach slingback for an emergency tube.

I shrugged. "What's it to you, De? Is *moisturizer* even going to be on the vocabulary part of your do-over test?"

De grimaced while applying Origins Precipitation corrective to my cheeks. "Let's don't, Cher."

As random schoolmates buzzed around us, Murray jumped in. "We've got to talk to you."

Letting De do her repair job, I sniffed. "Except in rare instances, you've brutally rejected my sincere overtures ever since Test Result Day. Excuse me for not thinking there was anything more important in your universe than your little do-over test."

The minute that came out, I felt a stab of guilt. The test *was* important. De's crash-and-burn performance really was devastating.

To his credit, Murray ignored my snide remark and stayed focused. "This is about the Jake dude."

Sean shook his head, murmuring, "The dude with a 'tude . . . the man with a plan . . . Jake the rake, the flake, the snake . . ."

"*What* are you babbling about?" I demanded, my eyes flashing. Sean's rap skills, while normally worthy, were merely annoying right now.

De looked me straight in the eye and cut to the chase. "We think Jake is bogus."

I was so stunned, I burst out laughing. "You do? And what amazing powers of perception did you use to come up with that?"

Sean said earnestly, "Well, for one thing, Adam looked him up. Jake doesn't go to UCLA like he said."

I couldn't believe I was hearing this. "Adam looked him up? When? In his spare time? Isn't the moonlighting munchkin way too busy for that? And, thinking caps, people: Jake's a transfer student. He might not be in the system yet."

De tented her fingers and elaborated, "That's the thing, Cher. Adam checked the registrar's office, the computers, he even looked up the names Jake mentioned as his professors. Nothing checks out."

I held my hands up defensively. "Why would you even be discussing me? I thought you were all studying diligently for the test. It determines your future."

Murray touched my cheek. "Cher, baby. Enough

with that. We care. So does Adam. After you left our tutoring session yesterday, it just came up. Adam mentioned that he isn't down with your Jake dude."

In spite of the cooling moisturizer, my cheeks were starting to burn. I tapped my foot impatiently and checked my Movado. "You know what, I have a life to get to. I'll catch you all."

De blocked my getaway path. Gently, she said, "Adam asked us what we thought about Jake."

"You all thought he was pretty amazing the other day when we had lunch together. That was obvious. I cite: Amber fawned all over him."

Amber started to contradict, but De interrupted. "Something's off about him, Cher. We all felt it, but it wasn't until Adam brought it up and we started comparing notes."

"Excuse me? You went biology one-oh-one and dissected my hottie—like some helpless amphibian in a petri dish?"

De said, "We put everything you told us about him together. And, Cher, it doesn't add up."

Bitterly, I spat, "Thank you, math goddess, but until you bring your PSAT arithmetic scores up, forgive me if I can't accept your conclusion."

Murray's jaw dropped. So did Sean's. Even Amber's—I heard the creak. No one had ever heard me diss De like that.

When I thought about it later, I realized that this was the Moment.

The moment in our relationship when De went beyond an eye shadow of a doubt and solidly proved her t.b.-hood. For instead of going all medieval at me as I deeply deserved, De put her arm around me and gently said, "Cher, taking a swipe at me doesn't change anything. This boy is not what he seems."

I felt like the air was liposuctioned right out of me. I whispered, "What is he, then?"

De gazed at me sincerely and admitted, "We don't know yet. But something is not kosher."

Just then the bell for next class rang. Lockers banged shut and our schoolmates scattered. But none of us made a move until Mr. Mazza strode by, demanding, "Don't you kids have classes to get to?"

Before he could actually check our schedules, Sean improvised, "We all got study hall now. We're on our way." And then my friends—and Amber—dragged me into room 119, which was currently unoccupied.

That's where the real interrogation took place. Sitting by myself in the front of the room, I felt like I was on the witness stand in a David Kelley TV show like *The Practice*. Or *Ally*. Although if I had to choose which David Kelley heroine I'd be, I'd pick his wife, Michelle Pfeiffer. I was busy picturing myself as actress-mom-Hollywood-wife Michelle, so I didn't hear opening arguments. When I tuned in, it was like this "trash Jake" free-for-all.

Murray, pacing in front of the blackboard, started. "The dude claims to be from San Diego, right? So, why, when we had lunch in the Quad the other day, did he pronounce coffee, like 'caw-fee.' Only in New York do they do that."

Amber leaned toward me and noted, "And only in

New York is walking an accepted form of transportation. Besides," she snorted, "that watch he had on? Hello, faux TAGHeuer."

I yawned in her face. "Go release some toxins, Amber."

But she continued. "Where'd he take you after Starbucks? Curry in a Hurry? Fill Ya' Belly Deli?"

Murray and Sean, what a surprise, found that howling-worthy. This time De did not stop them. Instead, she added fuel to the fire. "It does seem like every place he takes you is free of charge."

Amber added, "He probably thinks free-range chicken refers to the price."

I folded my arms across my chest defensively, refusing to divulge. I'd fully sworn to keep Jake's financial status secret. Instead, I went indignant. "What are you implying, that he has a fiscal duty to prove his devotion?"

Amber looked shocked. "Well, duh."

I ignored her to concentrate on De. "I allow that's what *you* need—your horoscope even said so. But for a boy to win my heart, materialism isn't the only way."

De rolled her eyes and snorted. "Earth to Cher, this is me you're talking to. I'm not quibbling about the romantic aspect of moonlight strolls and the beach at sunset, but the occasional meal at the Ivy sustains us. And a solitary sunflower is sweet, but two dozen long-stems is what signifies long-term."

I sighed. "Swing and a miss, De. Of all people, I expected you to understand. Jake is not just any random date flavor of the month. He's my destiny and my fate and my soul mate. And not that I owe you an explanation, but he happens to be embroiled in a totally temporary cash-flow snafu."

Amber concluded, "He's cheap, Cher. Either that, or he's a poseur."

De perched on the corner of my desk and took both my hands in hers. I knew she was going for empathy, but I pulled away. "There's something else, Cher. Remember when you sent in those personality profiles for the Love-O-Scope seminar?"

"We had to submit them for our personal charts. I simply—and efficiently—pulled all the information about us off our Web sites. What's that got to do with anything, Dionne?"

"Maybe nothing," she allowed. "But on your Web site, don't you have stuff like the Beach Boys is your favorite group? And that you love romantic movies. And that Acura is your dream car . . . and sunflowers are such bodacious buds . . . and that you're committed to human rights . . . *and* you take your lattes double decaf?"

I was livid. "Enough! What are you saying, De? That somehow Jake looked me up on the Internet? And then came into my life from out of nowhere, brilliantly disguised as my soul mate?"

Those words no sooner tumbled out of my mouth when I remembered Jake's favorite song, "Brilliant Disguise." Instantly, I squashed the thought: I refuse to inhabit that mental landscape. Like, why would Jake do that?

Swiftly, I gathered my books, bolted vertical, and

stomped out of the room. I barely heard De going, "Cher, don't be mad. Just be careful."

The concept of waiting for De to drive me back to Grandma's did so not appeal. But when I called for a cab, the address I gave wasn't in Santa Monica. Like ET, the alien, not the TV show, I needed to go home. "2232 Karma Vista Drive," I instructed the driver. I called Grandma from the cab and told her my plans. While disappointed, still she urged, "Go make up with your father."

By now it surprised me not that instead of Daddy being home, Adam was on site. I tried to sneak in undetected and slither upstairs, but the clicking of platforms on marble tile will always negate silence.

Besides, intern boy had a message. All apple-cheeked innocence—as if he hadn't been investigating my hottie!—he said, "I was hoping that might be you. I just took a message from the Beverly Hills Body Shop. Your car is ready."

I lit up. Vehicular deprivation ends! And like, not a moment too soon. All the improvising I'd been forced into lately had taken its toll. Not least of which was on my credit card for all the taxis I'd been summoning lately. Yet I was about to call for another when Adam offered, "Need a ride over there?"

Before I could respond—I was thinking of ways to phrase "like I *might* be seen in your car" creatively—he added, "I could really use a break. These files are starting to give me a headache."

On the ride over, I avoided polite banter with Adam.

Instead, I filled the silence with happy thoughts. Like: "In a short while, Daddy will see that Jake so lived up to his insurance-providing duties. My car will be fully paid for. And Daddy will have to rethink his knee-jerk distrust of my hottie."

Or not.

As soon as I spotted my Jeep, shiny as an Isaac Mizrahi lurex tube top and furiously unbent, I ran over and gave it a hug. "Welcome back," I purred. "Did you miss me?" Then I stuck my palm out and politely demanded the keys from Hal, the body shop Barney.

Tragically, Hal had a demand of his own. Payment.

I went indignant. "No way! What are you trying to pull? I know you got paid. Jake said so."

Hal matched my indignant and raised me a "how dare you." "You callin' me a liar? I run an honest business. I ain't been paid, and I got the paperwork to prove it. Here—see for yourself!" He shoved some random papers in my face, but no way would I examine them. He could have written anything on them.

I totally stood my ground. I demanded the keys to my car.

Hal totally stood his. He refused to hand them over without a check.

We might have remained at the impasse, but Adam stepped in. "Could I see the paperwork?" After scanning it, he looked up uncertainly. "These papers, uh, prove that the body shop tried to contact San Diego Chargeurs, the insurance company Jake Forrest gave them. Only they weren't successful."

Stubbornly, I said, "Why? Because they didn't even try?"

"Because it doesn't exist, Cher. It's bogus."

"Let me see that!" I grabbed the papers out of Adam's hands. But the words on the printout only confirmed what Adam had said. The body shop had made every effort to contact the San Diego Chargeurs.

Hal growled, "Like I said, girly. No check, no car." He started to turn away, but Adam stopped him with a tap on the shoulder. "Wait. I'll handle it."

I blinked. "You'll handle it? It's like five thousand dollars, Adam. Aren't you the starving student who can't pay for a turkey sandwich? Or something?"

Adam bit his lip. "Mel authorized me to use his credit card. For anything relating to the case or for emergencies. I think this qualifies as the latter." He turned to Hal. "What's the total?"

"Exactly five thousand eight hundred thirty dollars. Including the deductible."

That's when I learned that in cases of car repair, deductible is an antonym. It means an added expense.

I so did not want to ponder the implications of Daddy allowing Adam use of his credit card. Nor the implications of Adam bailing me out. Instead, I insisted, "There has to be a logical explanation for this." I pounded on the redial button of my cellular. But Jake never picked up his phone. And his voice mail wasn't accepting any more messages. It was full.

When I hopped in my Jeep, I watched Adam, just ahead of me, make a left in the direction of my house. I turned right—toward Doheny Drive. I had to find out why Jake hadn't taken care of the car. There had to be a reasonable explanation. My hottie, my soul mate, would not leave me stranded like this.

But stranded was how I felt fifteen minutes later, when I rang Jake's doorbell repeatedly. No one answered. I checked under the doorway. No light emanated from the apartment. Maybe Jake had stayed late at school to study. And maybe Sandy was . . . I didn't know *what* Sandy did.

By the time I got home, Daddy's car was in the driveway. Sure that Adam had babbled about Jake and the insurance fiasco, I steeled myself for a serious showdown. But Daddy met me at the door with outstretched arms and a warm, loving smile. It signaled one of two things. Either Adam hadn't had a chance to tell him what happened, or intern boy had exercised discretion. Again.

Daddy was pumped at my return. He hugged me, explaining, "Grandma Ray called me at the office and told me you'd decided to come home. I'm glad. I missed you. We'll talk later, but first I have a surprise."

As soon as he led me inside, I realized what it was: the aroma gave it away. Daddy had been cooking? "After I heard from Grandma, I was suddenly seized with inspiration. I made my specialty. Spaghetti with meatballs—plenty for all of us." Anticipating my protest, Daddy added in a teasing tone, "Just testing, Cher. You'll be very proud of me. They're turkey meatballs."

They weren't half heinous, either. Or maybe I was

just famished. Or more likely, fully panicked. I totally inhaled like half a dozen as I tried to figure out a way to tell Daddy that *he'd* paid for repairs on my car. And that I had no explanation from Jake. Yet.

In my head I tried out a bunch of famous phrases like, "When it rains, it pours. Would you even believe that there's been another mix-up?" Or, "It doesn't look good now, but it's always darkest before the dawn."

Daddy intuited my aggro. "Cher? Honey? You seem preoccupied. Is something wrong?"

I focused. Both he and Adam were staring at me. I affected casual. "Nothing. What makes you think—?"

Before they could answer, the doorbell rang. I jumped out of my seat. It was Jake. How could it not be Jake? With a check to pay for the car. With an explanation. With—omigod—the answer to Daddy's case!

"Baby!" I shouted excitedly as I flung open the door.

But the eyes that met mine were not cobalt blue. They were steely gray. And beyond flabbergasted. For never, in all my seventeen years, had I once greeted Officer Krupke with quite that level of enthusiasm.

He turned Barney purple and pfumphered, "I guess you were, um, expecting someone else."

"Good guess," I responded glumly as I turned around and headed inside. He followed, lamely explaining, "I'm sorry, I should have called first. But I need to talk to Mel. I was on my way home and figured I'd stop by."

Suddenly, I lost my appetite. I pointed to the dining room. "Daddy's inside. I'm going upstairs."

But Officer K's words stopped me before I hit the first step. "Cher? I think you might want to hear this. It's about that accident you had a couple of weeks ago."

Wrong. I did so not want to hear about it. None of it. Reluctantly, I trailed him into the dining room. Daddy seemed surprised to see his officer bud. He introduced him to Adam and invited him to join us for dinner. But Officer K had just come to deliver his "disturbing" news. Only because "we're friends, Mel."

Even though I'd told him not to bother—that Jake and I would handle it, Officer K had gone way above and beyond-y investigating my hottie.

"I ran a computer check on the license and registration info he gave me. I dunno why, it never seemed right that the kid didn't have a current registration. Or license. I mean, even if he was new in the area . . ."

The lines on Daddy's forehead deepened dangerously. Even Adam the ravenous put down his fork, paying rapt attention.

"I went with my gut, and it took a while to put it all together, but I was right. The kid falsified information."

I was steaming. "Not even."

Daddy shot me a stern look, but Officer Krupke seemed apologetic for what he was about to say. He bit his lip.

"I'm sorry, Cher. I know you like this guy. But nothing checked out. The car isn't registered to any Jake Forrest. In fact, the computer can't even find a Jake Forrest. Not at the address he gave me—which, by the way, turned out to be bogus. There is no Forty-third Drive in San Diego. Anyway, I figured the kid lifted the car, so I put the ID number through a search. But no one reported it stolen. It's leased, actually. Registered to an Alexondra Heller."

Heller. A flash of white-hot panic gripped me. The bell that went off in my head was nothing compared to those that went off in Daddy's. And, if ickiness could get worse, Adam's. He's the one who found his voice first.

"Mel? Cher? Uh, maybe we'd better go into the study."

Chapter 11

Over the course of the next hour, I got an earful—two, even—about the heinous Heller case.

Pacing the floor, Daddy took it from the top. "When I was in law school, my best friend was Bobby Heller. A brash kid, like me he was from New York and had no money. A lot of smarts, but talk about a schemer! Bobby always had an angle for everything. He managed to rig the pay phone so he made calls for free. Finagled a way to use the meal plan without paying. He'd buy clothes, leave the price tags on, wear them, and then return them. Talked his way into free tickets to rock concerts—then scalped them. Stuff like that."

Daddy paused, remembering. "I kind of turned a blind eye because I liked him. He was my roommate. And he held an honest job. We both worked as waiters to pay our way through school. We used to talk about opening a law firm together. We'd argue about whether to call it Horowitz and Heller or Heller and Horowitz. And of course, where we'd practice—New York or LA. If only he hadn't messed up, that would have been our biggest problem . . ." Daddy trailed off.

I tried to picture this Bobby Heller. Clearly, he had some connection to Jake. Nervously, I whispered, "So what happened?"

Adam answered. "The bar exam happened, Cher. The test that—"

I rolled my eyes. "Hello, I know what the bar exam is. It's like the PSATs. A post–law school über-test. If you rock, you pass go and collect big bucks as an attorney. If you tank, you're toast."

Daddy corrected me. "Most people who fail the boards take them over again. No one really wants to throw away three years of law school."

I knew that. A picture of JFK Jr. flashed before my eyes—hadn't the hunk taken it multitimes before passing? I ventured, "Bobby Heller failed?"

Daddy sighed. "Just the opposite. He passed—with flying colors, even."

I was confused. "So, how did the bar exam mess up your partnership plans?"

"The test didn't. *He* messed up our plans and, worse, his own life. Bobby cheated, Cher."

Daddy drew a long breath, then continued. "The test is divided into two parts. The first is two hundred multiple choice questions. The second is the essay portion. A few months before the test, he started dating this girl, Darlene Griffin. At the time, I couldn't figure it. She wasn't his type. She had different interests, different goals in life. Not like any girl he'd dated before—or even talked about."

Daddy shook his head, sighing deeply.

Adam picked up the thread. "Of course, she did have one thing no other girl had: access to the answers of the multiple choice part of the bar exam. She worked for the company that printed the answer sheets."

My hand flew to my mouth. "She gave him a copy of the answers."

There was more. Daddy delivered it. "Bobby couldn't let it go at that. He bribed some computer genius from the engineering school to hack into the system and get hold of the essay questions in advance. Let's just say that Robert Heller was more than prepared for the California State Bar Exam."

Adam added, "He wasn't discovered right away, so he figured he'd gotten away with it. He got a job as an assistant with an Orange County law firm. Your father scored a job right here in Beverly Hills. He and Bobby were still planning to practice together after they'd made some money and gotten some experience. But then it all fell apart. Two years later Darlene got engaged—to a minister. The girl had a crisis of conscience and turned Bobby in."

Daddy shook his head, grimacing. "At that point, if he'd just gone before the Office of Attorney Ethics and admitted cheating, the whole thing might not have gotten so out of hand. But he kept trying to fight it, denying any wrongdoing, even in the face of irrefutable evidence. The case eventually went to trial. Which it never should have."

"He lost?" I guessed.

Daddy nodded. "Big time. By that time Darlene contacted the computer hacker. So it came out that he cheated on both parts of the test. He got disbarred. It was awful."

I shifted uncomfortably on the couch. "But what did you have to do with it, Daddy?"

Quietly, Adam explained, "Your father defended him, Cher."

My jaw fell. "You did? How could you? You knew he was guilty . . . didn't you?"

Daddy plopped down on the wing chair, out of steam. "In my heart I guess I did know. But because we were friends, he asked me to defend him. I couldn't turn him down. I defended him pro bono—I used all my resources but eventually we lost."

Adam glanced at Daddy worshipfully. "When it was over, your father tried to help Bobby. Even though Mel still didn't have much money, he offered to take out a loan so Bobby could get his life back together—move to another state, let some time pass, take the bar all over again."

My eyes welled with tears at Daddy's loyalty. And goodness. Softly, I repeated, "You offered him a second chance. A do-over."

"I did, but he turned me down. He was just so bitter. He couldn't believe he'd gotten caught. It was really rough times. Because by then he'd gotten married to your mother's sorority sister Alexondra. They had a child. A boy named Jacob."

Okay, so no one had to connect the dots for me. I did it myself. Alexondra. The one Grandma Ray mentioned: the hanger-on. For which a common nickname is Sandy. She and Bobby had a boy named Jacob. My Jake.

Daddy went on. "Bobby and his family moved back to New York. Your mother and I, of course, stayed here. I tried to keep in touch, but he never responded. I finally gave up. I figured, eventually, he'd reconnect. In a million years, I'd never have believed he'd choose this way to do it."

"This way?" I repeated in a daze. What I'd heard was grievous enough. The news I was about to hear, I intuited, was worse.

Adam delivered it. "Bobby never forgave your father. He devised a scheme with the full cooperation of his wife to exact revenge. He's brought a suit against Mel."

"On what grounds?" I demanded indignantly, leaping off the couch and getting in Adam's face as if he was the plaintiff.

Adam stayed calm. "Bobby's claiming that he wasn't the only one who cheated. That Mel had the answers too. He's saying that out of some kind of twisted loyalty, he didn't come forward for all these years. But now, he says, his conscience is bothering him." Adam grunted. "Yeah, right."

"But it's all bogus!" I sputtered, and began to pace.

Daddy stood up and put a reassuring arm around

me. "Of course it is, Pumpkin. But right now it's his word against mine. He's saying that I only agreed to defend him for free so he wouldn't drag me into the case. He's saying my defending him was, in effect, extortion. Worse, he's contending that he has proof: a letter I wrote admitting I was in on his scheme. Now the whole thing may go before a disciplinary committee and maybe even to trial if I can't prove somehow that I wasn't in on it."

"A trial? With heinous negative publicity? That would be unthinkable, Daddy. Your A-list, all-star clients would lose faith in you."

"It's worse than that," Adam interjected. "Bobby's been contacting everyone connected with cases Mel has lost. He's urging them to sue for false representation. Your father's practice could be ruined. That's why we've been digging so hard to find proof that Mel was never in on Bobby's scam."

Daddy added, "It's been incredibly labor-intense. The Hellers have had a lot more time to put a case together. From what I can figure, they've been at this for over a year, poured every resource into it."

Something else was buggin' me. "But what do they have to gain? Bobby was found guilty of cheating. That's not going to change, even if . . . even if . . ." I trailed off. I could not go there.

"That's the sick part," Adam reported glumly. "We're not really sure. They're suing for damages— that Bobby took the complete fall for something they did together. But mostly, it seems to be straight

147

revenge. Anger. We've been researching Bobby Heller. It seems he never got back on his feet. We can only surmise it's been eating him up that Mel became so successful."

I didn't say it, because we all thought it: and so publicly. I flashed on that issue of *People* magazine. It was hardly in Jake's car randomly.

"They don't just want to disbar your father, Cher, they want to ruin him. That's why the case is so complicated. And," Adam added, "that's why he didn't want you to help. He didn't want to scare you."

Suddenly, Daddy went from thoughtful to seething. He banged his fist on the desk. "That Jake kid! I knew he was fishy! He's using you to get to me! I can't believe Alex would use her own kid! On second thought, people don't change. She'd use anything."

Daddy reached out and squeezed my shoulder pads. "I know you were hurt, Pumpkin, but it's lucky that I didn't let you help out. Imagine if you'd actually known the details of the Heller case. Imagine if that Jake kid did!"

The chunks burned my throat as they shot up with lightning speed. I felt each and every turkey meatball threaten to spew all over the plush carpet in Daddy's office. Without thinking, I grabbed the Hermès hankie out of Daddy's pocket and smothered my mouth with it. I took the stairs two at a time and, after slamming my bedroom door, called the only person I could.

De barely recognized my voice. But instantly, she understood. This was a mission for Super T.B.—and she'd better make it fast. I was totally choking. The minute I saw her pull into the driveway, I dashed out the door. I never said a word to Daddy, who shouted after me, "All you all right? Where are you going?"

De hadn't planned on an early evening rescue. I could tell by her ensemble, which fell under the heading Sweat Suit Chic. And her hair, which was still wrapped in a swirly thick terry cloth towel. She'd just gotten out of the shower and had not stopped to blow dry.

"Thanks, De," I said gratefully as she peeled out of the driveway. "This is a major props. But I've just ruined Daddy's entire life."

De jerked her head in my direction, shocked. Unfortunately, she also jerked the car, and we hit the curb. She threw it into park. "This is about your father? Not that Jake?"

White knuckled, I gripped the dashboard. "Don't you mean, 'that snake'? Oh, De! You were right. I was so blind. He's fully bogus. And he's after Daddy. And I . . . I aided and abetted."

De closed her eyes and let out a long breath. "Wait a minute, Cher. Whoa. We'd better go somewhere. We'd better get backup. This sounds beyond Emergency Nine One One." With that, De got on her cellular. She called Sean. And Amber. And told them to meet us around the corner at Murray's house.

Over the course of the next half hour, in Murray's downstairs den I went through an entire box of those designer pop-up tissues. And chocolate. For the minute Murray got De's frantic "we're on our way" call, he stocked up on crisis essentials. I was midway through my third Cadbury bar and my twelfth chorus of that famous hand-wringing whine "What am I going to do?" when Murray abruptly left the room. I thought he'd gone to get more supplies, but not even. When he returned, he explained, "I called Adam. He's on his way over."

I exploded. "How could you do that, Murray? He's going to tell Daddy—before I can figure out how to fix this."

But Murray didn't agree. "Adam's a good guy, Cher. I know you don't like him, but he really is on your side."

Sean added, "Mur's right. Besides, Adam's the only one who knows what's in the files you gave Jake. You don't. We don't. Maybe the damage isn't as bad as you think."

I shuddered. "Or maybe it's apocalyptic."

De put a comforting arm around my shoulders. "Adam may be the only person who *can* help right now. Over the past few weeks in his tutoring course, we've gotten to know him. He's a righteous dude, Cher."

"Penniless, of course," Amber had to sniff. I was too distraught to ask why the fashion waste was even here. Unless she and De had bonded over bad PSAT scores. Yuck. Another place I didn't want to go. So I returned to the whine cellar. "Adam's just Daddy's new golden child. And he thinks I'm the biggest ditz in the world."

"No I don't, Cher. Really. How could I think that? You rocked the PSATs, didn't you?" Although Adam— who'd apparently flown around the corner to Murray's—said that totally without guile, I was livid.

I spun around to stare straight at the khaki-clad kid. "A career in stand-up does not await. Your timing stinks."

But it was that famous French phrase: *au bon pain*. Or *au contraire*. Or something. Because Adam's timing was stupendously stellar. As was—and it piqued me to admit it—his clear head. His analytical thought process. His inclusive instincts. And he'd brought paper. After assuring me that he hadn't breathed a word of my major leak to Mel, he totally took charge. "Okay. Let's write down everything we know. From the day you met Jake. Everything you told him. Exactly which files you let him copy."

During the next hour, Adam gently grilled me. I admitted that I'd told Jake, like, everything I knew about Daddy's cases. I'd thought he worshipped Daddy. And wanted to be just like him. And wanted to help. As if!

Adam refused to believe that I was the only one who'd spilled pertinent info. "Think, Cher," he implored. "The two of you spent a lot of time together. I just bet Jake accidentally told you something we could use."

I sighed. I racked my brain—the left and the right side—recounting every conversation Jake and I had. But the only thing that came to me was all the deceptions. Everything Jake had ever said was a lie—except one thing. The part about "Brilliant Disguise" being his favorite song.

I was feeling sorry for myself and addendum, unbelievably stupid, when it came to me. I slapped Murray's dad's desk. "I do know something that might help. But it didn't come from Jake."

Everyone looked at me expectantly. I stood up. "Anyone hungry?"

My t.b.'s exchanged "Cher's got mad cow disease" looks. De even tried to feel my head for fever, but I brushed her hand away.

"We, my friends—and you, Adam—are making a pilgrimage to the condo of cholesterol-overload. We're going to Grandma Ray's."

We piled into Amber's second car, her Range Rover—the only vehicle big enough to house all of us. Even then De sat on Murray's lap. On the way there, I explained. "When I took refuge chez Grandma, she told me that Mom wrote letters to her about these old cases. I don't know for sure, but knowing Ray—and the relationship she had with Mom—I bet she saved them all. And if we're lucky? Hello, Bobby's using a bogus letter as proof that Daddy was in on it—maybe we can find a real one that proves he wasn't."

Chapter 12

Luck was mine. Grandma Ray *had* held onto every last bit of correspondence from Mom. She'd kept it all in a trunk in her living room. Most of it dated back to the early '80s: the Heller case decade.

Naturally, Grandma was pumped to see me. She was more excited to see my friends. "You're all too skinny," she decreed. Then, sizing up Adam, amended, "Except you."

And even though it was like, ten o'clock, she whipped up a full five-course cholesterol fest. De, Murray, Sean, and Amber gleefully partook as Adam and I fully rummaged through all the archival correspondence. And authenticity alert: just like the stuff they dredged up from the safe in the *Titanic,* it was all readable. Dusty, smelly, and wrinkled, but totally decipherable.

Adam spread Mom's letters out across the bumpy

Berber carpet, quickly organizing them by week. With each batch, his smile grew wider. His chaotic curls bounced with glee as he bobbed his head, declaring, "We've struck oil, Cher. It's all here. I have to take all this back and comb through it—but this looks like our best shot at proving Mel had no knowledge of what Bobby did."

Grandma piled several wrinkled shopping bags on Adam. "Here, use these to take the letters. Don't lose anything. I expect it all back in one piece."

Adam assured her he'd return every last missive. He wanted to bolt and go through the cache, but Grandma wouldn't hear of it. "Just because you're not a skinny melink doesn't mean you couldn't use a *bissel kugel.*"

The looks on De's, Murray's, Sean's, and even Amber's faces, as they happily stuffed themselves was all the endorsement Adam needed. He caved. But not before insisting, "Only if Cher's having, too."

I shot back, "Only if you let me help you go through this stuff. I refuse to be left out again."

It was post-Conan late when we got home, but Daddy was still up. His eyes went wide when he spied Adam schlepping all those shopping bags. "Where've you been? You look like you're coming from . . . Ray's house?"

Miraculously, Adam convinced Daddy to go to bed while he and I worked in the study. Daddy seemed dubious. But I guess at this point he trusted Adam. And not that I'd admit it to the law drone, but Adam had fully earned Daddy's trust. And mine.

Working together, it didn't take us very long to unearth what we were looking for. It was the pre-cellular and E-mail era, and Daddy had communicated with Mom by letter. Grandma's cache included the total stash. She'd saved not only Mom's letters to her, but Daddy's to Mom.

In those private missives, some clearly penned late at night, Daddy went fully confessional. He described what he'd been going through. He was so torn! His head was spinning about the cheating scandal. At least three letters contained the phrase "You think you know someone—but you don't." Many more expressed Daddy's total dismay because Bobby didn't need to cheat. Daddy believed that Bobby could have aced the bar honestly.

He wrote, "I lived with the guy, so how could I not have seen the signs? He was always trying to get away with something. And now I'm defending him. There's so much I can't use in open court, because it will make it worse for Bobby. I'm lucky I have you to act as a sounding board."

Daddy was such the soul searcher! What he felt most bummed about was that he wished he *had* known—he would have talked Bobby out of it. But he'd loved Bobby like a brother and been blind to his cheating ways.

Just as I'd been blind to Jake's.

As I read the last letter aloud to Adam, he gazed at me with admiration. "This should do it, Cher. These letters will hold a lot of weight in exonerating your father. Obviously, he forgot he even wrote them. And obviously, when compared against the bogus one Bobby has, they'll—"

". . . prove his innocence, won't they, Adam?"

"They prove more than that, Cher. They prove he's a good man, too. Smart, loyal, caring. Not unlike his daughter."

I grinned. "So I guess this cancels out anything Jake may have found in the files I gave him. I mean, we did it, didn't we, Adam?"

"No, Cher, you did it."

Awkward moment alert: if Adam had been, well, anyone else, I would have hugged him. But it was hard enough for me to even stop resenting him. So I just said, "Should we wake up Daddy?"

Adam cocked his head. "I'm gonna guess he never went to sleep. He had to know something big was up."

I should have been beyond exhausted, but I remained sleep-challenged. After Adam and I told Daddy, I called all my friends. I gave them, even Amber, major snaps for their speedy and unconditional support. Naturally, they all said it was nothing—except Amber, who'd spent the evening devising ways for me to thank her more concretely. We settled on my Narciso Rodriguez cashmere sweater set.

The rest of my buds asked for only one thing in return: would I please bring a case of antacid to school tomorrow? Grandma Ray's kugel was causing major tummy turbulence.

I should have felt completely pumped. Daddy's case, and his career, were saved. My buds were back. Correction: they'd never really been gone. But as I tossed in bed, totally wrinkling the silk sheets, all I could think about was Jake.

And how, if I was such the PSAT-rocker, could I have been such the dunce to miss every sign. When I thought about it, Jake had a left a trail of them as wide as Rodeo Drive.

Like, the no-insurance thing; the magazine in the car. And if he was really from San Diego, he would have known about LA's Griffith Park—and not been so stoked at the plethora of palm trees. There had been so many New York references! Like Radio City, the Rockettes, the way he slipped and said "caw-fee" as Murray had astutely pointed out. And hello, Bruce Springsteen! "Brilliant Disguise"! Jake as much as *told* me he was faux.

And yet, I believed. I just wanted to so badly. De had been right all along. Her add-'em-up math skills were stellar. She deserved to rock the PSATs.

I didn't want to go to school the next day, but Daddy insisted. "We'll take it from here, Cher. But don't worry. I'll tell you everything that happens."

Over the course of the next few days, Daddy made good on that promise. He decided not to contact Sandy—Alexondra, that is. There was no reason. Entering the old letters as evidence was enough to make the whole bogus lawsuit go away.

Daddy wouldn't even press charges. "What good will it do? It'll just make it worse for her. And that son you seemed to like so much."

Daddy is still such the mensch. He hasn't changed

at all. It taught me a wholly important life lesson, which I shared with my t.b.'s the day they retook the PSATs. "A mere test score doesn't determine your whole future. Who you are as a person determines it. And you guys—my t.b.'s—are the best. No worries."

Daddy didn't want me to ever contact Jake again. But I needed closure. So one day after school I drove to his apartment. Like why was I not surprised to see a moving van outside? I hoped I wasn't too late. I rushed up two flights of steps and rang the bell.

Jake was taken aback to see me. When he opened the door, he turned a bizarre shade of green that clashed with his eyes. I could tell immediately that Daddy had wasted no time setting things right. And that Jake knew everything. Still, at first, he tried to dodge my ire.

"I came to tell you what a jerk you are. Tibet doesn't need poseurs like you."

Jake pleaded, "Wait, Cher, it's not what it seems."

"No, Jake, it's not. It's worse." I paused. "You once said we could tell each other everything. So, like, riddle me this. How did you expect to get away with this? Did you think I wouldn't eventually figure out that you had no insurance? You had no money? You probably don't even care about Tibet!"

Jake slunk back into the apartment and went confessional. "It wasn't supposed to unravel this quickly. It's true, we hadn't been paying our bills lately, because we used all our money on this—"

"Scam. It's okay, Jake. You can say it."

He grimaced. "That's not the way my father explained it. He said we needed to get back what was rightfully ours. . . ." Jake's voice trailed off.

"And you believed him?"

His eyes were downcast. "He's my father, Cher. What can I say? Anyway, we never had any money. We used everything to appear wealthy. To lease that car you love so much, to rent this Beverly Hills apartment and buy these bogus clothes." He stopped, snorting, "Which, honestly, I would never wear in a million years. I shop at Old Navy, by the way."

Involuntarily, a picture of Adam flashed before my eyes.

Jake continued, "We needed money to come to LA. My dad stayed in New York because we could only afford two tickets. The credit cards weren't supposed to have been canceled that fast. And the car accident thing? That really was an accident. I'd been following you for a few days, but you were always surrounded by people. I couldn't get you alone. I meant to just tap your car—I never figured there'd be that much damage. I never figured a cop would stop—let alone a friend of your family's. We'd stopped paying our car insurance, but even so, I didn't expect the policy to run out that quickly. When I found out that it had, I gave the body shop a phony name in San Diego. At that point, I was just stalling for time. And then, of course, something else happened completely unexpectedly. I really fell for you."

"As if!" I totally stomped my foot. "You have nothing to gain by lying now, Jake. The gig is up. You got all this info off my Web site, didn't you? That's how *my* favorites rapidly became yours. You never even liked the things you said you did. I mean, hello, do you even like sunflowers? Or Acura sport utes? Or . . . or . . . double-decaf, light-froth lattes?"

A trace of a smile—talk about inappropriate!—flashed across Jake's chiseled cheeks. "No, no, and no," he admitted. "And definitely not the wussy Beach Boys. I'm a Billy Joel man. With a New York State of Mind." The way he said it, "Noo Yawk," hurt my eardrums.

I added, "You just reinvented yourself to connect with me. You never even liked me."

He held his hand up. "That's where you're wrong, Cher. I mean—right, but ultimately wrong. It all started just like you said. We saw the article in *People* and the part about you having your own Web site. I went on-line, and I used a search engine to find it, though you can't imagine how many sites are still devoted to that singer! Anyway, I did pretend to be the guy of your dreams. I cop to all of that. Only, like I said, a weird thing happened during the past few weeks: I really started to fall for you. And I'm sorry, Cher. I hope you can find it in your heart to forgive me someday."

"Don't hold your breath, Jake."

As I turned on my heel to march away, I tossed one more question at him. He answered honestly: he wasn't even an Aries.

Daddy wanted to have a big celebratory dinner, just the two of us. I insisted on inviting Adam. I knew it would be a treat for him. And, hello, he so deserved it.

We all went to Wolfgang Puck's Café, where Daddy and Adam fully gorged on chicken parmesan. I stuck with seared ahi tuna.

When we got home, Daddy invited me into his study. He and Adam were putting away the old files and did I want to help them?

I begged off, citing homework. But that wasn't the real reason I headed up to my room and closed the door. I had something of major importance to do: I went on-line and erased all the personal stuff from my Web site. Not that I thought anyone else would pull the kind of scam Jake and his family had. But, whatever: a Betty can't be too careful.

Even after everything, I refused to be cynical. I still believed. I believed in astrological signs, my horoscope. And I so believed that the one person for me, my soul mate, was out there.

I wondered if the stars were shining—could I see the Big Dipper or was it enshrouded in smog? I opened the set of French doors that lead from my bedroom onto my terrace. I stepped outside. The air, while humid, somehow felt good on my face. Moisturizing.

Suddenly I heard, "Bye, Cher."

I looked down. Adam was loping toward his I-Don't-Care-mobile, and waving at me. "See you tomorrow."

I'll never know what came over me. But suddenly and totally unbidden, I heard myself calling to Adam's retreating back, "What sign are you?"

Adam never turned around. He simply raised his hand and yelled back, "Aries."

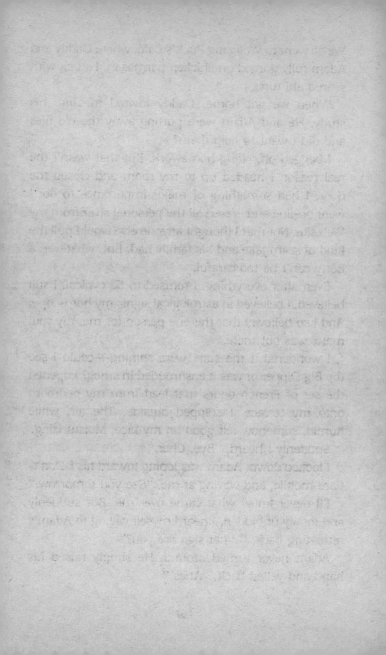

About the Author

Randi Reisfeld is the author of the *Clueless* novels *Chronically Crushed, True Blue Hawaii, Too Hottie to Handle, Cher Goes Enviro-Mental, Cher's Furiously Fit Workout,* and *An American Betty in Paris.* She has also authored *Prince William: The Boy Who Will Be King, Who's Your Fave Rave? 40 Years of 16 Magazine* (Berkley, 1997), and *The Kerrigan Courage: Nancy's Story* (Ballantine, 1994), as well as several other works of young adult nonfiction and celebrity biographies. The *Clueless* series, duh, is totally the most chronic!

Ms. Reisfeld lives in the New York area with her family. And, grievously, the family dog.

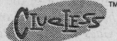

What's it like to be a witch?

Sabrina The Teenage Witch™

"I'm 16, I'm a Witch, and I *still* have to go to school?"

◆◆◆◆◆

#1 Sabrina, the Teenage Witch
by David Cody Weiss and Bobbi JG Weiss

#2 Showdown at the Mall
by Diana G. Gallagher

#3 Good Switch, Bad Switch
by David Cody Weiss and Bobbi JG Weiss

#4 Halloween Havoc
by Diana Gallagher

#5 Santa's Little Helper
by Cathy East Dubowski

#6 Ben There, Done That
by Joesph Locke

#7 All You Need is a Love Spell
by Randi Reisfeld

#8 Salem on Trial
by David Cody Weiss and Bobbi JG Weiss

#9 A Dog's Life
by Cathy East Dubowski

Based on the hit TV series
Look for a new title every other month.

From Archway Paperbacks
Published by Pocket Books
1345-07

Published by Pocket Books   1491